A Wolf in her Way

ANNA KATMORE

To Jack.
My Wolf.
I can't believe
I didn't notice you for so long.

Whispering Pages

Book 2

Chapter 1

Eighteen hours earlier…

Jack

Riley escaped to the land of dreams hours ago and now sits cuddled against my chest, drooling on my shirt. The warmth from the fire in the stove is so soothing and enticing that my eyes drift shut a couple of times, too. But I refuse to nod off, even though the grizzly bear skin that we settled on is quite cozy. Instead, I replay the day with her in the Wood of 1000 Dawns again—especially the parts where we built the hilarious prince trap together and fooled around in the haystack behind the mill. I enjoy listening to her soft breathing way too much. It's calming. Reassuring.

And deceiving.

It's so easy for me to pretend that Red Riding Hood and the big, bad Wolf have a real chance at love...just the way we are.

Riley doesn't see that happening. Not because she doesn't like me. Oh, I know that she does. She's proven it several times over the past couple of days—like when she spent the night sitting with me in Phillip's dungeon or took me on a hunt through the woods afterward. The moment I turned back into myself at her granny's house, she was in my arms. And nothing has ever felt better than that.

But for little Miss Red Riding Hood to fall in love, it takes a prince—at least that's what she keeps telling me. Romance only happens among royals. Her analysis of the love stories here in Fairyland doesn't permit any other conclusion. Every romantic fairy tale has either a prince or a princess in it. Since Riley and I are neither, we can't have a sweet ever after together. For her, I'm just the guy who always eats her granny at the end of our story.

And frankly, I am. Or...I was. So many years, so many times playing the same tale over and over... And I never saw who she really is. Never knew what a funny, adventurous, and sweet spirit actually dwells beneath that red cloak. She isn't just the character that I want to eat for a couple of hours every day while we're playing anymore.

Now, she's the girl who means the world to me.

I don't want to lose her to someone else. I don't want to give up my place in our story. We belong together—always have, and always will. And if I have to turn into a prince to make her understand that, then by the end of the rainbow, I will.

All this past week, she's been making plans to get her happily *ever after*.

Last night, I made my own.

At the crack of dawn, I carefully lift her off me and settle her down on the bearskin. She stirs, and I tense like her drawn bow. If she wakes up now, her pleading gaze as she begs me to stay and accompany her to the ball will trap me. Her deep sigh a couple of seconds later, however, assures my escape without notice.

Her cloak still hangs on the chair near the fire where I put it when we came in yesterday. It was soaked from the downpour that caught us unawares as we kept watch on her prince trap. The crackling fire dried it overnight, and now, it feels wonderfully warm as I grab it and carefully drape it over her. Riley snuggles into it with a tender expression. Instead of my t-shirt, she's drooling on the bearskin now. With a smile, I brush a silky brown lock away from her face.

Then I rise, walk to the front of the hut, and open the door. A thick blanket of gray fog silently creeps around the house and brings a chilly breeze into the room. I cast a glance at Riley on the floor. She doesn't seem to feel the cold. Her eyes are still closed, her expression peaceful. The sight triggers something inside me. Maybe I shouldn't leave without a word? But even if I can't tell her about my plan, I can at least say goodbye and give her an excuse for my disappearance.

Quietly, I close the door again and start looking through drawers for something to write a message with. In the living room, I find a pad and several pens in an askew chest, and sit down at the table to scribble a few words.

Dear Riley,

I need to run an errand outside town, which can't wait. I'll be back in a few days. You'll have to tell me everything about the ball then.

Good luck with the prince hunt!

In a zestful line, I sign with my name and leave the note on the table for her. As I push back the chair and rise, the legs scrape traitorously across the floor.

"Jack?"

Sucking in a sharp breath at her mellow voice, I freeze on the spot. Nothing more follows. As I turn around, her eyes are still closed. She hasn't really woken up, only mumbled my name in her sleep. Hopefully, it's a nice dream. Maybe one about us diving into haystacks again.

I look down at her for another long moment. Part of me longs to wake her and say goodbye before leaving, but it's better this way. Easier. I'm lousy at finding excuses.

What I do, however, is add another line to her letter.

P.S.: Sorry for not waking you, but you looked extremely adorable drooling on the bearskin.

Then I sneak out the door, change into the Wolf, and start running through the foggy morning.

My first stop is the prince trap. If a prince really—however ridiculous the idea might be—sleeps on that bed of pillows, I'll either have to eat him or scare the shit out of him so he never again sets foot in the Wood of 1000 Dawns. Red Riding Hood is *not* going to ride off into the sunset with some damn royal.

A snore ahead raises my hackles. What the hell? There can't really be...? Lifting my muzzle, I sniff. No, not a royal. Their blue blood always has the distinctive note of aged paper to it, which I can't detect now. But if not a prince, then who?

Curiosity draws me closer until I smell something entirely different. I don't even have to sneak all the way over to the camp to know what it is. A dwarf. Breakfast is canceled.

Inwardly laughing, I shake my head. Riley is in for a surprise when she comes to check later. Damn, I wish I could stay and watch the spectacle, but I have other plans. More important ones.

Leaving the short man where he slumbers, for I'm sure he means no danger, I sprint out of the forest and into town. Some of the early risers crossing my path—probably heading to the bakery—jump out of the way in terror. Their eyes wide, they press their backs flat against the wall of Goldilocks' beauty parlor and let me pass. Sometimes, my reputation comes in handy.

Only when I turn into Honeypot Square do I change back into myself and head up the stairs of a two-story building. A fingerprint scan lets me into my apartment. I had Bob the Builder change the lock a while ago when the Cat and the Fox broke into Geppetto's workshop twice in one month.

After a night in Riley's cramped and cozy house, entering my sparsely furnished studio apartment feels like walking into a naked cave. The couple of shelves hanging on the white walls don't hold any whimsical items. If anything, they're just something to collect dust. The dark sheets on my chrome-framed bed don't look inviting anymore, and the plain kitchen with its blue-fronted cabinets hasn't been stocked with food in ages. The pub is just around the corner, and I've never been passionate about cooking.

I take a quick shower in the small bathroom and then pull on my black leather pants. They should do for my plan. I hope Phillip can provide the rest. His walk-in closet is massive compared to my little one. Slipping on a black hoodie for now, I leave my apartment again and bolt through the woods on four paws once more because it's the fastest way to my best friend's castle.

This time, I deliberately avoid the path from Riley's house to the trap. She's probably out and about by now.

Back in human form, I cross the stone bridge to the castle gate and use the giant doorknocker in the shape of a rose with a ring. Phillip and Rory's aged grand butler, Edgar, opens and welcomes me with his gray, weed-like eyebrows drawn into a condescending scowl. As usual, his white hair is braided down his back. "Master Jack. What an unexpected visit at this time of the day." His nose wrinkles as he inspects my outfit. In his own creepy way, he all but tells me to turn around and come back later, maybe after he's swallowed his happy pills for the day.

It would have been so much easier to get past this point if Phil had opened the door, or even Rory. But it's probably too early to expect either of them downstairs.

"Eddie, old boy!" I smack the stiff servant on the shoulder and brush past him with a grin. In the entry hall, I wait while he closes the door then brushes away a non-existent speck of dust from his black tailcoat, precisely where I just touched him. I roll my eyes. "Could you ring Phillip out of bed, please? This is an emergency."

"The prince and his wife have been up for a while," he informs me, leading the way to the grand stairs. Once there, he turns around and freezes me on the spot with only a glare.

A grin pops up on my face in answer as I innocently clasp my hands behind my back, rocking on my heels. "You know what? I think I'll just wait here."

The arch of his right eyebrow tells me where I can shove my humor. Damnit, no one in Fairyland speaks as clearly without words as this pestilent butler does. Why Phil and Rory keep him on is beyond me.

Edgar climbs the stairs with the slowest ascent ever. No doubt he's doing it on purpose. We haven't been warm with each other from the beginning, and have never made a secret of it. I don't believe the butler knows a temperature above zero actually. But I might have plummeted on the scale of esteem in his books the day he saw his niece Gretel walk out of my apartment. Yep, reputation doesn't always come in handy.

I wish there was a way to shoot him faster up the stairs, though. At this speed, I'll still be waiting here at noon. Bored, I let my gaze trail around the hall. On a gold-leafed chest next to me, there's a picture of Phil with Aurora under a tree. A vase with pink roses looms next to it, and a mobile of the moon and several silver stars hanging on invisible cords from a stainless steel cross loosely balances on a stand. After a brief glance at Edgar to make sure his back is to me, I nudge the moon and then give the whole cross a gentle shove so it turns on the pointed tip.

"I'd rather you not touch that," the butler's grumpy voice drifts down the stairs.

My gaze snaps up to him, but he's still ascending, one hand on the rail…facing forward. Shit! How does he do that? I swear the thing made no noise, and it doesn't appear that he turned around.

Pressing my lips together in annoyance, I lower to the bottom step and wait like a nice little boy.

"Jack!" Phil's worried shout and the hurried footsteps on the stairway behind me a couple of minutes later make me jerk to my feet. He slows down when he catches a glimpse of my face. "Oh, good! You look...yourself." He adjusts his favorite red shirt that hangs casually over his blue jeans. "When Edgar said there was a wolf problem downstairs, I thought I had to put you in the dungeon again."

I cock an eyebrow. "Well, isn't your butler blessed with the charm of a Harpy?"

Phillip laughs. "Don't screw his niece, and he might be a little nicer to you."

"I haven't laid a finger on her in years." The cold edge disappears from my tone as my best friend reaches the bottom of the stairs. "Happy birthday, buddy." I pull him in for a quick, brotherly hug then cast him a sincere look again. "Anyway, I'll never touch another girl besides Riley again if my plan to romance her works out. And therefore, I need your help."

Phil stares at me for five thunderstruck seconds before he shakes his head and narrows his eyes. "There's too much confusing information in that sentence." He grabs my arm and drags me into the parlor. "Let's have breakfast first."

He closes the sliding doors, securing us some privacy in the room dominated by several yellow-upholstered sofas and chairs grouped around a coffee table in front of a gold-framed bar. The wall across the way is decorated with a variety of weapons—swords, rapiers, crossbows, anything a young man's heart might desire. A pool table in the back of the room rounds it all up nicely, and the floor-to-ceiling windows grant a marvelous view of the palace gardens.

Phil's choice from the shelf is not a cup of coffee but a bottle of scotch with a label that says it's seventy-eight years old. A fine aroma drifts out as he uncorks it and pours us two glasses, handing me one.

"Cheers." We clink glasses, the ice cubes bobbing in the amber liquid, and I take a sip. Phillip demolishes his drink. He wipes his mouth, puts the glass down, and rakes a hand through his hair. "Now what was all that about romancing Riley?"

I slump down on the noble sofa, clasping my drink in both hands between my spread legs and watching the ice swim. "She's gone completely insane about finding a new ever after."

"I figured that out last time you came here."

My gaze slides to him leaning with his back against the bar, ankles crossed and fingers wrapped around the edge. "I can't let that happen. We belong together." Lips compressed, I pause for the length of a breath. "I don't want to lose her. She's all I've ever had." If anyone can understand what's going on inside me, it's Phil. "She's the one for me."

A moment passes in utter silence. Then the damn

prince throws his head back and explodes with laughter. "Jack Wolf is falling."

With a wry glance at him, I lift my glass in a toast. "As I live and breathe." Then I down the drink.

When Phil gets a grip on himself again, he eyes me with intrigue. "And how exactly can I help you?"

Placing my empty glass on the small table in front of me, I rise and walk toward the bar. Face-to-face with Phillip, I solemnly tell him, "I need you to turn me into a prince."

His brows narrow half in confusion and half in amusement. "Dude, I'm not the lost son of the Fairy Godmother."

"Not with magic." Determined, I put my hands on his shoulders. "I have a plan."

Chapter 2

Jack

Phillip sits across from me and scrutinizes me over the small table between us that holds a half-empty bottle of a seventy-plus-year-old scotch, along with two refilled glasses of the amber liquid. "You're absolutely sure it's not the aftermath of Jekyll's elixir that's clouded your senses about Red Riding Hood?"

"Are *you* sure you didn't only fall in love with sweet Aurora because of your father's verbal beatings when you were still single, and he wanted to marry you off?"

"Good question." He laughs as he stands because the

little bell by the door of the parlor chimes again for the third time within the past half hour. The cord attached to the bell runs upstairs, straight into Rory's chambers. From what Phil told me earlier, she broke her leg yesterday and now has a cast. Obviously, she can't flitter around the castle while preparations for the ball are in progress, so she's taken to summoning her prince every so often with new orders.

As he leaves the room, I call out, "Phillip?" He turns near the door, and I send him a serious look. "I *am* sure."

After a second, Phil nods. "We got this covered, pal. Don't worry."

Sounds of chatter drift to me. Curious, I take my scotch, rise from the sofa, and stroll to the tall window. There, in the garden, the house staff is hanging up lanterns, decorating the trees and the stone statue of a rising unicorn near the pond—Rory's favorite animal.

Two heavy knocks on the front door echo through the castle, making me whirl around. Although I'm curious, it's important that no one sees me here today. Even Edgar was told that I left again after a quick chat with the prince.

Since the parlor is Phillip's retreat, none of the servants will walk in here without being summoned. And Princess Rory is occupied in her room, having her hair done and preparing her costume for the ball. Besides, she can't walk downstairs without help, so we're safe. She's the last person who should know I'm here because her hotline to Riley will ruin my plans.

The door slides into the wall, and Phil returns, bringing company. This one I don't mind at all. With a wide smile, I walk over to Eric, and we bump fists. My brows draw up in delighted surprise. "What are you doing here?"

"Ariel is driving me crazy because of the feast tonight." Groaning, he shrugs out of his leather jacket, which he's wearing over a white *My ride is a mermaid – what's yours?* t-shirt, and tosses it behind the bar. "She's tried on twenty-seven different gowns in the past couple of hours, and each time, she forced me to tell her why I like the damn dress better than the one before." He shakes his head as he pours himself a glass of brandy and knocks it back. "The woman's gone berserk."

Obviously beat, he sinks into Phillip's vacated chair as I reclaim my seat on the sofa. "I checked in at the *Shady Wonders* to see if one of you was there, but the pub was empty. And since you weren't home either, Jack, I came here." Feigning a whiny baby face, he looks at Phil. "Please don't send me home again."

A wry grin on his lips, Phillip claps Eric on the shoulder as he walks past and sits down next to me on the sofa. "You're in luck, then. We need another accomplice."

When Eric lifts his black eyebrows in confusion, we quickly fill him in. I would love to say that he took the news with more sobriety than the blond bastard next to me, but that would be a lie. Eric laughs his head off, then downs another inch of liquor and laughs some more. With my friends' total ham reactions, it's getting a little clearer now why Riley doesn't see me as a potential happily ever after.

Eric eventually calms down and meets my misery with the necessary sympathy. He leans forward, claps his hands, and then rubs them together. "So, what's the plan?"

"First, we're going to make a prince of Jack," Phil informs him. "We need to change his looks enough so no one recognizes him." He sends me a sly sideways glance. "And, of course, you need to learn to dance, buddy."

Yeah, I was afraid of that, but to play my role perfectly, I'll prance around. Pressing my lips into a thin line, I give him a sharp nod.

"Later, at the ball, I'm going to court Riley," I tell Eric. My brows waggle. "Incognito. She won't stand a chance against my undeniable charm."

Eric whistles through his teeth. "So you want to make her believe you're Prince Two-Face of Dreamland when you meet. And then what?"

"Prince Jacob of the Snow Plains, actually," I correct him. "And then I'll show her that it's not only a blue-blooded dude who can give her what she's looking for. At the end of the ball, when her heart is finally hung up on me, I'm going to tell her the truth."

"Risky plan. But it could work." One arm folded over his chest, the other elbow braced on it, Eric taps a finger on his lips. "Your hair color has to change. Your eyes, too—if that's even possible. Are you going to wear a mask?"

I nod. Phil has one for me.

"Yeah, you absolutely must. And you also need to shave. I guess there's nothing we can do about your stature. A cape maybe?"

"Mm-hmm. Riley needs to see from a distance that I'm a prince. I'll be wearing one of Phillip's royal uniforms. Oh, by the way"—I jump up and rush to take down a rapier from the display on the wall—"I want one of these, too. It'll perfectly round out the outfit."

"You don't even know how to handle a rapier." Phillip laughs at me. "You'll end up killing someone with it." He always enjoys riling me up about being below him in fighting prowess. But he's trained me too well to actually believe it.

Faking a mean face, I slide the blade under his chin and lift it up a little. "You better stop laughing, or that *someone* is going to be you."

Another rapier flies past me, and Phillip catches it in his right hand. I didn't see Eric getting up and grabbing it from the wall. Skillfully, Phil knocks my weapon aside and comes to his feet. "You have no chance."

Grinning at each other, we engage in a mock battle of life and death in the middle of the room.

A series of swift metallic clangs rings out. And exactly as he's drilled into me day after day in the arena, I hold my left arm away from my body and only concentrate on the fighting hand. With a wicked sneer, I attack, moving forward step by step. Phil retreats, stepping backward onto the small table that gets in the way.

"Guys! The scotch!" Eric blurts out and makes a dash for the bottle before Phillip can knock it over.

The next obstacle is the sofa. Luckily, Phil doesn't mind boot prints on the cushions. Easily, we overcome that, too, and battle on solid ground again, stubbornly trying to draw a point by poking each other. Hah! If he thought he'd have it easy with me, he was in for a surprise.

In the middle of our fight, Rory's little bell chimes out…again. A frustrated frown mars Phil's face. *"Argh! What do we have servants for?"*

He swings his rapier two more times, and suddenly, mine goes hurtling out of my hand. My mouth hangs open as I track its progress, flying in an arc toward him. The bastard catches it in his left hand, then rotates both hilts around his fingers like they're guns, gripping them backward. With a bout of force, he stabs them down into the table, embedding the pointed tips deep in the wood. A smirk makes his blue eyes gleam. "Game over."

My eyes narrow to annoyed slits. "Damn! How did you do that?"

"Told you I'm the better fighter." He chuckles and heads to the door. As he slides it open, a few maids flitter by with more lanterns, big bows of light blue satin, and countless white and pink roses in their arms.

"Phil," I call out after him and wait until he turns. "I want a rapier tonight anyway. And bring a sack of flour when you come back."

When it's only Eric and me in the room, I face him where he stands by the bar and lift a brow. "You need to teach me how to dance."

He chokes on his sip of brandy. "Now?"

"Yes, while Phillip is gone. I'm not going to have any dude watching while I'm dancing with another."

His face scrunches in thoughtful lines. "Good point." He puts the glass away and comes forward, sliding a quick look to the closed door. Then he begins to explain. "So you put your right palm to the small of my back, and take my hand with your left."

Yikes, it feels weird to be this close to Eric. But I swallow my unease and do as he instructs.

"Good. Don't slouch. Keep your spine straight and your eyes focused on your vis-à-vis." He instills the right posture into me and then commands, "You start with your left foot backward. Right foot backward and to the right, and then the left foot closes to the other."

Looking down, I move my left foot back and place the other like he showed me while Eric mirrors all my moves forward.

"Eyes up, dude. If you watch your feet while dancing at the ball, everyone will think we picked you up from under some bridge." He laughs.

I don't. This is hard. I've never danced before.

Eric instructs me to do the same movements forward now, starting with my right foot. Man! Can't I just sway Riley a little on the dance floor? How will I ever get this rhythm into my head?

We repeat the moves a couple of times until Eric seems mildly happy with my progress. "These are the basic steps of a waltz. Once you have them down pat, start adding a slight swirl and widen your steps."

I begin to do that when the door opens. As if zapped by lightning, we leap apart in a panic, glaring at Phil as he enters.

He stares at us, his mouth shifting into a smile as he ponders. Slowly, he puts the small sack of flour he brought onto the table between the two rapiers that still stick in the wood, and then meets our flaming faces. "Did you two just make out?"

"Not funny," I growl, sitting down on the sofa again. "Eric was teaching me how to waltz."

Because this situation is more than uncomfortable, obviously not only for me, Eric quickly asks, "What did Aurora need?"

Thankful for the distraction, I lift a curious brow at Phil.

A moan escapes the tortured prince. "She wants to mark a path through the castle with tea lights. From the entrance to the ballroom." He smacks his hands over his face. "The little monster's going to burn down my home."

"Girls," I say. Eric laughs, adding, "We live to make them happy, don't we?"

Phil's fingers move up to tug at his hair. "And where the heck do I get fifteen hundred candles from anyway?"

Eric and I exchange a look, then shrug, and say at once, "At Lumiere's."

Resigned, Phillip walks to the door, opens it a crack, and calls out, "Edgar! Saddle the mare. I'm riding to Grimmwich." He throws a taunting glance back at us. "And you two, don't get too intimate while I'm gone."

"No, we'll hold off on the good parts until you get back," I drawl out in a voice dripping with sarcasm and flip him off.

But, of course, we don't wait. I want this dancing thing done before Phil returns. Eric gives me some more instructions and, thankfully, lets me dance on my own then, humming a tune and correcting my posture every few seconds. An hour later, I think I have the hang of it. The steps flow quite naturally, and I don't have to permanently look down to watch my feet anymore.

Eric grins, obviously happy with my progress, too, and hoists himself onto the bar. He nods toward the sack of flour still sitting on the table. "What do you want with that?"

"Ah, right!" I pull the cords open and dip my hand inside. "It's for my hair." Running my flour-coated palm across my scalp, I cast him an expectant look. "What do you think?"

Impressed, he tilts his head and studies me. Then he slides down from the counter and walks around me, inspecting my hair from all possible angles. "Not bad, actually. It looks a little powdery, but the color is definitely different."

I crack a sneer, waggling my eyebrows. "The powder will just give me that aristocratic touch."

"True. You won't stand out among those powdered wigs that I'm sure some of the guests will be wearing tonight." Then he folds his arms over his chest and chuckles. "As long as you don't walk in the rain. Otherwise, you might start a whole new fashion with a clump of dough on your head."

"I don't think it'll rain tonight." A wave of enthusiasm rising inside me, I dig both hands into the sack and finish the new style of my hair with more layers of white.

Phillip returns just then, halting by the door for a stunned second when he sees me. "Awesome, dude!" Grinning, he comes closer and holds a small pack out to me. "And look what I brought you."

"What is that?" I take the small box and inspect it.

"I made a detour to Dracula's place on my way home. That's why it took me so long."

I cast him a wary glance. "You didn't knock out his teeth and put them in here, did you?"

Phillip rolls his eyes. "I knew he did something to his eyes whenever he comes out of his tomb to mingle. Usually, they're flaming red, but when he's out and about, they always appear oddly normal."

I never knew that Vladimir's true eye color was anything other than blue.

"So apparently, this is what he uses to disguise them.

He called them contact lenses. You put them into your eyes, and they make the irises look blue."

"Put them into my eyes?" My face shrivels, and a feeling of uncomfortable foreboding overcomes me. "How?"

"Yeah, about that..." Phillip mirrors my uneasy expression. "You won't like it."

My stomach slides to the floor.

He points me to the chair and takes the pack away from me as I sit down. "Lift your face and open your eyes wide."

Because I do as instructed, I can't see what he's unpacking. But the queasy feeling in my gut grows fast as he leans over me and stretches out his finger. It looks as if he's going to poke my eye out. "What the—*fuck*!"

In a panic, I jump from the chair and try to squint away the debris he put into my left eye. Except, no matter how much I rub or blink, it stays. "Shit, that burns!"

"Keep your eye closed for a few minutes and don't move it," Phil commands. "Vlad said that'll help. You need to adjust to the thing. Once you stop fighting it, the pain won't be so bad."

I throw myself onto the sofa and try to lie still on my back. The reflex to rub the thing out of my eye doesn't disappear, though. It's the hardest battle of mind over matter I've ever fought.

"Are you ready for the second one?" Phil asks.

"No."

My protest hits a wall. He's over my face again, prying my good eye open. Shit, I hate him! There's another lens on his finger, but this time, he doesn't get to poke me because, in reflex, I shut my eye and seal it closed.

"Eric," he says in a commanding voice, and the next thing I know, my lid is forcefully opened. The finger comes, the lens sticks to my eyeball, and I curse in pain.

They give me a few moments to adjust again. While I struggle to keep my eyes closed and remain still, tears trail down the sides of my face. Eric's voice sounds from somewhere to my left. "How does it feel?"

"As if you put pins in my eyes."

Phillip's chuckle resonates, amplified by the glass he must be holding to his lips. "No pain, no gain, dude."

Still lying on the sofa, feet dangling over the armrest, I turn my head in his direction and frown, but I take care not to open my eyes. "You're enjoying this, aren't you?"

"Just a little bit." He pauses, and there's a clank as he puts his glass away. Then his stupid laugh follows. "Hey, Eric? Do you think Riley will like to hear that Jack cried because of her?"

I groan, draping my arm over my face. "Fuck you, you son of a king!"

They keep making jokes at my expense for several minutes. At some point, I don't even listen to them anymore. Behind closed lids, I start to move my eyes just a tiny bit. When that feels okay, I roll them some more until it feels safe to open them. The pain is only minimal now, like when the wind dries out my eyes while running. I blink a couple of times and then sit up. Everything around me looks slightly blue, but it's not too bad.

"What does it look like?" I ask the guys as I turn to them at the bar.

Both princes stare at me with open mouths. Eric runs a hand through his hair and finally calls out, "Shit! Jack—You're sporting Smurf eggs!"

I grin. Sounds like success.

While Phil runs up to his sweetheart with lunch, I use one of the downstairs bathrooms to shave with a borrowed razor. It feels strange to run my fingers over my clean-shaven skin. I can't even remember the last time I walked out like this. On the plus side, Riley has never seen me like this before. Only the mask is missing now. With the white-powdered hair, my new noble, clean jawline, and the brilliant blue eyes, Riley certainly won't recognize me.

I sneak back to the parlor, presenting myself with a confident grin to Eric, who nods his approval.

At the same moment, a low thud on the door makes us jerk around. "Open. It's me," Phil's voice drifts through the wood.

Confused, I rush to let him in. He carries snacks on a plate in one hand, and a pile of clothes in the other. When he sees me, he backs away a step but then quickly shakes the surprise from his face. "Damn, you look young without the dark stubble." He walks in and puts the things on the bar then turns to me again. "But it makes all the difference.

Not even I would realize it's you at first glance."

"Man, the food comes at the perfect moment," says Eric as he opens the buffet. I take a look at the other things Phil brought while munching on a sandwich, too.

The dark leather boots with flaps remind me of the ones D'Artagnan used to wear. They excellently match my leather pants. There's also a white uniform jacket with silver buttons in two rows down the front and some intricate silver embroidery on the chest. The band collar and cuffs are light blue satin. I slip on the boots and jacket, flexing my shoulders and walking a few haughty steps across the room. Everything fits perfectly.

Phillip holds out a silver mask with darker ornamentation. "Try this on."

It covers half of my face, from the tip of my nose up to my hairline. I tie the cords at the back of my head and then run my fingers along the edges.

"Amazing." Eric whistles. "Now, if you could only do something to disguise your voice, the masquerade would be perfect."

Right, my voice. That could turn into a problem. "But how should—"

My sentence breaks off when Rory's voice drifts to us, sounding much too close to the door. "Phillip?"

We all stiffen, and Phil sucks in a panicked breath. "The monster is up."

Shock roots me to the floor. Thank Grimm, Eric reacts much faster than I do and pushes me behind the bar.

I duck just in time before the door slides back.

"Phillip, are you in here? You need to try on your costume," the princess calls. Then a startled "oh" follows. "Eric. I didn't know you were here."

"Yeah…" he stammers, and I can clearly hear the unease in his voice, which is certainly for my sake. He gives a sheepish laugh. "I took flight from Ariel. She went a little over the top because of the ball."

Aurora giggles. "I guess we're all a little excited today." A smack sounds out, like a clap on someone's arm or shoulder. I try to spy through the glass door of the cupboards, but I can't see what's going on. "Phillip, you should have told me that we had a guest. Eric could have eaten lunch with us."

"You ate in bed," Phil's dry voice sounds out. "I'm not bringing another man into your chambers."

"I would have come downstairs into the dining room, silly." I can almost detect the eye-roll in her deep sigh and have to bite back a chuckle.

"Don't worry, I'm fine here," Eric assures her. "Your husband brought some snacks. That's more than enough. And I have to go home, anyway. Ariel is probably waiting."

A moment passes, then I hear Rory again. "All right. I'm looking forward to seeing you two later at the feast. And *you*"—that certainly means Phillip—"come up for the costume." The clacks of crutches on the floor and a limping thud move away from inside the room back to the door. Fortunately, she didn't notice me.

"Love?" Phillip stops his wife, and I hold my breath again. "You know the story of The Wolf and the Seven Young Kids, right?"

"Mm-hmm."

"What does the Wolf do to change his voice before he comes to eat them?"

"Hmm…I think he eats chalk."

A shudder rushes through me at the thought.

"Why do you ask?"

"Ah, just a little bet between Eric and me," the prince lies sovereignly. "He insisted it was salt, but I knew it couldn't be that." The smack of a quick kiss echoes. "Now, rest your leg, sweetness. I'll come upstairs in a minute."

As she leaves the room and the door slides closed again, a stream of air finally whizzes out of my lungs. *Phew*, that was close. I climb to my feet, coming out of my hiding place to face my friends.

They both grin at me like freaking loons.

With a moan, I tip forward, fold my arms on the bar, and bury my face in them. "Please…don't make me eat chalk."

Chapter 3

Jack

The soft chatter of voice drifts to me in the brightly illuminated ballroom that's slowly filling up with guests. "This looks great."

"The juvenile hoarseness fits your baby face," Phillip, disguised as a phantom in a black hooded cloak, jokes as we stand together by the pyramid of champagne glasses.

Earlier, my friends forced some chalk down my throat, and they were rolling on the floor. But no matter how desperately I coughed and choked as a nasty layer of dust coated my vocal cords, it did what Aurora promised. My voice lost its darkness. Sadly, I sound like a teen Wolf going through a voice change now.

With a grin, I pat the rapier attached to my hip. "I have this to make up for it."

Phillip carefully shifts the white mask diagonally covering his face and sips his drink. I don't. The liquid would just wash away the chalk dust from my throat, and I really don't want to force down another handful of it before I meet Riley.

The big grandfather clock situated in the corner next to the stairs shows nine o'clock. A frown creeps onto my face. The string quartet on the dais has been playing for over an hour. "Where is she?"

"Calm down, pal. She'll come." Phil claps a hand on my shoulder. "Cindy said she had some troubles with her outfit, but they found a solution. Riley will be here soon."

Nervously, I watch the staircase and the entrance above. Her closest friends are gathered around a seated, invalid princess by a long table decked out with a multitude of cupcakes. The girls seem as excited to finally see Red Riding Hood tonight as I am.

I sweep the ballroom with another glance. Maybe I missed her coming down the stairs, and the colorful sea of dresses and masks weaving around the place swallowed her up? With a sigh, I turn back to Phil. "I'll have a walk around. If you find her before I do, don't let her run off with another prince."

He laughs. "Promise."

But an uneasy feeling suddenly floods me and keeps me rooted.

"What?" Phillip demands.

"I don't know. It's just…" I shake my head. "If anything goes wrong—if I can't find her or don't get a chance to talk to her—tell her that she looks amazing when you see her. Because I'm sure she will."

He gives me a firm nod, and we head off in different directions. I continuously scan the ballroom for her. If Riley is already here, she can't be that hard to find. I stroll past the mighty columns situated symmetrically throughout the room. Beautiful tendrils of pink roses wind up the white marble. In between, there are rows of tables with a scrumptious feast set on silver platters. Hors d'oeuvres, sweets, pudding, and much more—the food looks simply delicious. But even if it wasn't for the chalk in my throat, I couldn't eat a single bite. My stomach has turned into a roller coaster over the past hour.

The amazing chandelier with its hundreds of crystal drops throws light around the room and over the pool right beneath, like sunrays playing on an enchanted lake. The pool houses countless goldfish that zip through the crystal-clear water. Above it, sits the glass platform that will serve as the dance floor.

Phil told me earlier about a request his wife had asked of him. Since she can't dance with her hurt foot, she wants him to show Riley off to the guests by opening the first waltz of the evening with her. I can't say that I like the idea. But if my girl has to dance with someone else, I'm glad it will be Phillip.

Of course, we honed Rory's idea a little as I practiced dancing for hours in the parlor this afternoon. If everything goes according to plan, Phil will hand Riley over to me before the song is over.

Since the stairs are still empty, I angle to the left and exit through the wide-open French doors that lead outside into the garden. The occasional couple sits on stone benches, while small groups of guests gather beneath the beautiful paper lanterns, displaying scenes of various tales from Fairyland. I stop and smile when I come across one with Red Riding Hood and the Wolf depicted on it.

Everything out here is just as magical as inside the main ballroom. Aurora clearly outdid herself with the preparations, even if she only directed them at the end due to her broken leg.

I amble around outside of the castle, jumping over a small line of bushes to get to the front. The scratch in my throat is annoying as hell. Perhaps it's safe to trust that Riley won't recognize me in this masquerade and just take a drink from the moat.

With great care, I skid down the grassy slope and try not to dirty the boots or Phil's uniform by falling. At the bank, I squat down and cup some clear water with my hands. Holy pixie dust! The first draught is a wonderful relief. It washes away the bitter taste of the chalk from my throat and makes me feel like I can speak again without breathing blue smoke.

Grating the small cubes of chalk from the pool table in the parlor wasn't Phillip's best idea today. They were meant to smooth pool cue tips, not my voice. Unfortunately, it was the only available chalk in the castle, and the guys' creativity got a little over the top. For the first couple of hours after testing Rory's theory, I was Puff the Magic Dragon.

I'm about to bring another draught of water to my mouth when a shadow races over the ground. It makes me look up to see what kind of giant bird just shot across the moon. Except…it's not a bird.

My chin drops. Water drips from my hands as my gaze fastens on the striking white horse descending from the night sky. Slowly, I rise and stare up at the stone bridge. Like the train of a wedding gown, the wondrous animal lowers its gleaming, white-feathered wings as it slows from a gentle gallop to a stop in front of the palace doors.

A girl slides off its back. Her gown is a bellflower dream of soft pink on top, deepening into a rose red at the bottom. Countless tiny diamonds sparkle around her waist and downward as the moonlight gives them each a tender caress. Tiny white blossoms are woven into her tied-up brown curls, but it's the innocent smile under her soft-pink eye mask that even the stars above cannot compete with that captures me. For a moment, I can't breathe because she's so beautiful. And her name is Red Riding Hood.

As if under the spell of her magic, I draw closer. With

a satin-gloved hand, Riley rubs the flying horse's forehead, mumbling a thank you that drifts to me. In that instant, the impressive beast shrinks to nothing more than a petite robin and flies away toward the Wood of 1000 Dawns.

She gazes after the bird for several motionless seconds. I nearly call out her name then because I long to tell her how truly stunning she looks tonight. The slip registers just in time, right before her name would have left my lips. I bite my tongue and simply marvel at the lovely girl while hidden in the shadows.

Riley turns around, smoothing her hands down the front of her dress. The deep breath she takes raises my compassion. I know she wanted me to come with her tonight—to escort her to the ball. Now, she has to face the society of royals on her own.

Her steps are hesitant, her look even shyer as she greets the two armed men standing guard outside the castle doors. They ignore her. Sure, it's their duty to face straight ahead and not get distracted by anything or anyone, but I wish they'd made an exception and at least returned her salutation, just to make Riley feel welcome.

When she disappears inside the castle, I sneak past her from a safe distance, keeping to the shadows of the walls. Even if Riley knows her way around these halls, there's absolutely no chance of missing the way to the ballroom tonight. All fifteen hundred candles that Phillip had to dig up today are now placed in two flaming rows that lead through the great hall and off to the east wing. I don't know how many roses the servants beheaded to litter the sides of the tea light path with so many petals.

Along the way, Riley tilts her head in every direction, seemingly in deep wonder. Two late-comers—the woman dressed in midnight blue, and her partner wearing a matching frock—hurry past, but it doesn't make Riley go any faster. The distance from the entrance to the east wing is only a couple of hundred feet, and yet it feels as if she's taking forever and a day to get to the grand staircase leading down to the ballroom.

The golden light at the end of the hallway gives me hope that soon I can start in on my plan to enchant her.

Phillip will dance with her.

I'm going to steal her from him.

She's going to fall in love with me.

And our ever after will be the happiest of them all.

But then Riley startles me as she stops and flitters to the side, finding shelter behind the thick, dark red curtains that frame the entrance to the ballroom. What the hell? Is she hiding from someone? It sure looks like it. But who? A guest?

For several moments, I silently scrutinize her from just around the bend. Hands clawing the red velvet, she tries to make herself as small and invisible as a girl actually can. Her shoulders tremble. And then it dawns on me. She isn't hiding from someone, she's withdrawing from the crowded feast itself. Only a few more steps, and she would be crossing the threshold to the ballroom. The point of no return. With the stairs now empty, and her stunning rosy dress a real eye-catcher, everyone in the hall will marvel at the grand entrance she'll make.

I lean my head against the wall as a sigh leaves me. "Sorry," I whisper…for not being there for her.

When Riley takes a baby step forward, I hold my breath, almost believing she's found her courage and will walk on. But she still clutches the curtains as if they're the only things in the palace that can guarantee her safety. If it wasn't so heartbreaking to watch, it would coax a smile from me.

As though I have no control over my legs anymore, they start moving toward her. Slowly and warily. I expect her to turn around any second and expose me, but the truth is, she doesn't even notice me as I stand behind her for several long moments.

Since there's no chance of sneaking away again and keeping to the original plan, I realize that some opportunities just have to be seized. Let's hope my voice plays along.

With a quick little cough to clear my throat, I straighten my spine, hold up my head, and ask in a soft but confident tone, "May I help you, milady?"

Boy, look at that! My voice is dark again but still raspy. Shouldn't be too easy for her to recognize me by it.

Riley swings around, her hand flying. I stiffen in fear that she's going to accidentally plant a punch to my jaw again like the other day on the prince trap in the woods.

Apparently, surprises don't work so well with her. Thank the leprechauns, she only clutches her heart this time.

Our gazes meet and lock for a seemingly endless stretch. I hold my breath. She can't know who I am. She just can't!

And she doesn't. There's no sort of recognition in her look whatsoever. I'm safe. *Phew*.

Eventually, her sweet mouth opens, and in a shy voice I've never heard from her before, she begins, "Um…no, thank you. I was just—"

When she breaks off, I help her out. "Scared of walking down?"

"Yeah. Maybe a little." Her lashes quickly shield her coy gaze, then she sends me a little smile. "It's my first ball of this kind."

I bet she doesn't even know how cute she is when she's opening up like this. It makes me want to be alone in the woods with her again. To banter, play, and jump into haystacks… But she just had to come here and find someone to write a different ending with, didn't she?

My head tilting to one side, I clasp my hands behind my back. I know exactly what kind of ball she means. The sort where she sneaks in and picks a husband from the royal prince buffet. Still, I feign ignorance and taunt her, "The *masked* kind?"

Obviously, it's too early for jokes. She gapes at me with big doe-eyes as if I just ripped the floor out from beneath her feet. Damn, I want to take her into my arms and tell her that everything will be all right.

For damage control, I try to ease her tension with a smile of my own. "You shouldn't be scared. You look amazing."

Her cheeks take on the color of her dress. "Thank you."

She's not used to getting compliments. Not the wild girl from the woods. In hindsight, I should have praised her more often because she *is* beautiful, even on normal days when she's skipping through the forest in her red cloak and dirty boots. It's those honey-hued eyes and her smile that make it all so perfect.

"Would you like me to escort you down?" I offer, hoping that I won't have to steal her from Phillip, after all.

Her eyes fill with insecurity. "That's very kind of you. But I'm afraid I need another minute."

Okayyy… So that means we're going to wait here together until she's ready. But from her wary gaze, I realize that her waiting time doesn't include me. "Very well." Back to the original plan it is then. I give her a polite nod, but I refuse to let her get rid of me so easily. My gaze lingers on her sparkling eyes, and the rasp in my voice lowers to a seductive drawl. "I hope I'm fortunate enough to catch a dance with you later."

It's more than a simple request, it's my silent promise to her.

Riley's eyes grow a little wider with surprise, and her delicate throat twitches as she swallows.

Right, honeydrop. The left corner of my mouth tugs up. That's how we're going to play this game tonight.

I turn on my heels and stride off. But before I head down the stairs, I slide a final glance over my shoulder to make my intentions absolutely clear. Riley's cheeks are red, yet her eyes gleam with shy wonder.

At the bottom of the stairs, Princess Snow-White, dressed as a black-and-silver-spotted cat, and the Beast's Beauty stand together, their arms linked, both scanning the place as if they're looking for someone. It's not hard to guess who. Avoiding eye-contact, I brush past them and quickly say, "There's a girl hiding upstairs behind the curtains."

In the turmoil of the feast, I'm not sure if they heard me so, a few steps farther on, I turn around and, with relief, find them heading up to the hallway. At least now, Riley doesn't have to come down to the ball alone.

Back in the ballroom, my gaze alights on Phillip in his dark hooded cloak, chatting with three others. Eric's disguise is being bare-chested, holding a trident, and wearing a shell-encrusted crown. His blue pants have fish scales all over them. He thought it would be fun to parody his father-in-law for all the times the merman made his life hell.

Okay, it does look hilarious.

With them are King Richard and Prince John, both wearing their usual robes but holding masks on sticks—each with the painted face of the other.

"Gentlemen," I call out in greeting.

Phillip introduces me to the two royals as his cousin, Prince Jacob of the Snow Plains. Frankly, when somebody else says the name, it does have a nice ring to it. He then leans closer and whispers, "Did you find what you were looking for?"

I nod and turn toward the stairs. They all follow my example just in time to see three beauties appear at the top. Days are rare when I don't see Princess Belle in her signature purple color, and Snow-White is known for her love of animals so, of course, she'd pick one to be her disguise. But the flower in their middle is unfamiliar.

The girls pull Riley downstairs much too fast for her to enjoy the wonders of her first royal ball. Her eyes glaze over with fascination. And mine do as well—probably like countless other men in the room.

Next to me, Prince John whistles through his teeth. "Shoot me, who is that girl in pink? She looks like a direct descendant of the Goddess of Virtue."

I cast him a disgruntled glare, which he doesn't notice because his attention is focused on Riley. "Queen of the Underworld," I snarl. "She's known to burn her lovers alive after she drags them to Hell." Then I add in a lighter tone, "Picked a great masquerade, didn't she?"

Snorting with laughter, Phillip claps a hand on my shoulder while Eric chokes on his drink and spins away so none of the others can see how he struggles to keep a straight face. Prince John throws me a look of horror. I tuck my hands into my pockets and grin.

My gaze skates back to Riley on the stairs. The girls still pull hard at her hands but, her face filled with awe, she stops halfway down. Hauled backward, Snow-White is fast to catch her balance. Poor Belle's high heels apparently don't allow the same agility. She trips backward, flopping on her behind and sliding down two steps.

I draw in a sharp breath and grimace. "Ow." That didn't look nice.

Half of the room joins me in pitying her, while Riley rushes down to her and helps her up. It's good to see that the sunflower can laugh about her slip and obviously didn't hurt herself. One princess with a broken leg at the ball is enough.

At the bottom of the stairs, the crowd sweeps the three of them away. "I'm sure they're taking her straight to Rory," Eric says.

The phantom nods and murmurs with a smug expression, "Let the show begin."

Prickling shivers race through me. I cross my fingers in my pockets.

Then Phil speaks loudly enough for everyone to hear. "Excuse me, I need to get this drink to my wife." His black cloak flaps ominously behind him as he disappears around the cupcake table.

Ariel throws a brief glance at him as she makes her way to us from a different direction. Her narrow, swan-feathered gown ends just above her ankles and, underneath, her naked toes peep out. That's not a big surprise—the mermaid is always barefoot on land.

"There you are," she says before planting a quick kiss on Eric's cheek. "I looked for you everywhere."

She turns to us, and Eric makes a formal introduction. "Darling, this is Prince Jacob."

I take her hand for a brief kiss. Lowering my head helps me escape her curious gaze.

Apparently, she knows Richard and John because she's not introduced to them. Ariel slips under her husband's arm and studies me with a little too much interest as the prince and the king try to engage her in light conversation. I cough and inconspicuously turn away. Sneaky, that one.

Fortunately, Phillip walks to the middle of the glass deck, and all attention in the room zaps to him. Jaws drop in surprise. Since everyone in here knows him and Aurora, their frown of confusion when they see Riley at his side is understandable.

"Good evening, ladies and gentlemen," he says, "and welcome to our ball." In respect, everyone briefly bows his or her head. I follow suit. "Because my sweet wife lost a fight with a root yesterday and broke her leg, the lovely Lady Riley has given me the honor of the first dance and will open the ball with me tonight."

Riley looks terrified. Her eyes zoom around the place as if high on caffeine. That eases when Phil gives her a reason to focus on him. He takes her in his arms and signals with a nod for the string quartet to start the music.

A mesmerizing waltz begins. It's the same song that I swirled light-footedly through the parlor to in training this afternoon. Again and again. I have every step down pat and know the exact moment when Phillip will give me a chance to nip Riley from him.

"Excuse me," I say to the others and walk closer to the dance floor.

Phillip does a great job of easing Riley's tension, and she looks as if she's starting to enjoy herself. I love her smile. It's captivating and almost makes me miss when Phil swipes his hand to invite the other guests to join him on the dance floor.

"Good luck, dude," Eric calls out as he and Ariel pass me, being the first couple to answer the request. Jassie and Aladdin walk onto the glass deck from the other side, but they're not the only ones. The space fills quickly as if swarmed by bees.

My nerves tighten. Half of the song is over. It's mere moments until Phillip will twist Riley away from him. I put one foot on the floor…

He's doing a test run of the move on the other side. I take two steps into the crowd, trusting that the oncoming couples will evade me. The second time he swings her far off his arm, they are passing me. Holding my breath, I fall into step, catching Riley right in the turn.

Her cheerful laughter cuts off immediately, and she stiffens like a pillar in my arms. Her head swivels away from me. She's obviously trying to find Phillip, who we left behind. The prince stands there for several seconds and, when our gazes connect briefly, I mouth the words "thank you" to him. He smirks in reply, and then he's gone, swallowed by the many dancing couples.

It's only Riley and me now and, after another extended moment, she finally looks at me. Her eyes sparkle like silver water tonight.

"What—in—who…?" In her apparent shock of finding me as her kidnapper, she doesn't get out more than that. I give her all the time she needs to gather herself, and it's nice to feel that, after the first round on the glass dance floor, some of the acute tension eases out of her body. "Why did you steal me away?" she demands then, her head tilted up and eyes narrowed behind the satiny mask.

I can't help but smile at her almost offended reaction. She's a fighter, always has been. And she takes shit from no one. "With over fifty gentlemen waiting to dance with you, I wanted to be the first."

"Well, you're hardly the first. The lord of the castle surprised me with the news of opening the ball with him three minutes ago." Her face scrunches with cynicism. "He's actually the one you stole me from."

No, I didn't. He played you into my hands, Red Riding Hood. "There are plenty of other fine women to dance with," I counter. "The prince can have his choice." To show her what I mean, I wave my hand at the couples dancing around us. "Besides, Phillip is my cousin. I'm sure he doesn't mind."

Seconds tick by, and she just stares at me. So cute… I lean forward to her ear and whisper, "I bet now you're surprised." My lips brush her skin, and it's almost impossible to withstand the urge to nip her earlobe.

Riley doesn't quite pull away, but I can feel her quick intake of breath since I'm holding her so close. With her lids lowered, she answers, "Maybe…a little." Then she dares me with a direct look into my eyes. "Shouldn't the *plenty of fine women* have worked for you, too? No need to rob your cousin of his dance partner."

I hold her stare. "None of the others interest me like you do."

"I…do?" she stammers, but she quickly clears her throat and adds a very formal, faked nonchalant note to her voice. "I mean…that is very kind of you, Prince…"

"Jacob of the Snow Plains," I reveal with a smug grin since she's so obviously fishing for my name.

"Oh, the Snow Plains." Her eyes widen with interest. "Aren't they far up in the Marble Mountains? It is said to be the most beautiful place in Fairyland's North."

I've never been there myself, but the stories people tell about the magical ice world are legendary. Of course, it would rouse her interest—that's why I picked it in the first place.

"It certainly is," I confirm as the waltz comes to an end, and we stop dancing along with the others. I let go of her hip but keep her hand in mine. With a gentlemanly bow, I brush a kiss to her knuckles, never breaking eye contact. "But not as beautiful as you, Lady Riley."

Her hand trembles a little in mine. I run my thumb across the back of her fingers to calm them before I straighten and send her a tender smile. "Would you honor me with another dance, milady?"

A surge of joy races through me because an answering smile lingers at the corners of her mouth. The ice is broken.

"I daresay it's my turn to kidnap the fair princess for a dance."

My head snaps around to the intruding voice of another man. Except what I find next to me is a damn chicken. Feathers of varying shades of brown and gray are stuck into his dark hair. They also cover the mask shielding the top half of his face, and he wears a bright orange linen shirt to complete the crazy farm style.

As he holds out his hand to Riley, hers slips from mine. What the hell?

I lance the intruder with a lethal scowl but, as usual with this kind of annoying fowl, he tries to take over the territory by fluffing up his feathers and firing a deadly glare back at me.

A muscle works in my jaw. The chicken better get lost before I pluck him.

The coward decides to escape my stare and moves Riley away from me, to the middle of the dance floor. A new song starts, and the two begin to dance.

Oh no, sucker, you're not getting away with my girl! My hand finds the hilt of my rapier as I start off after them.

But Riley's shocked look in my direction freezes me to the spot. Her glance drops to the sword attached to my hip, and when it shifts back to my face, the panic in her eyes is hard to bear.

I don't want to be responsible for her fright. This is her night, the big ball. I can't ruin it by starting a massacre on the dance floor…even if I want nothing more than to behead the barefaced chicken and have it for dinner.

He casts a snide look at me as he says something in Riley's ear, making me tighten my fingers around the hilt of my weapon so hard, I can barely feel my hand anymore.

The rooster is dead!

But Riley's gaze still clings to me, and whatever he said to her, it made her seem even more terrified. She's silently pleading with me now. And I can't just ignore it.

No matter how hard I try to stick with my instincts, after several seconds, I yield to her silent demands with a sigh and ease my grip on the rapier.

Then she's gone. The fowl has swept her farther away to the other side of the dance floor, the swirling couples aiding his dastardly intentions to hide her from me.

He's got my girl all to himself now.

Chapter 4

Jack

"Jack, dammit!" Phillip grasps my arm, forcing me to stop from walking through the French doors. "Why did you let her go?"

My plans to catch some fresh air and cool off ruined, I swing around to my friend. "Because it's hardly proper to bloody up the ballroom at your birthday celebration." Stealing his champagne glass, I down the drink, then my face hardens to stone. "Anyway, it seems as if Riley *wants* to dance with the fucking rooster, so who am I to ruin her fun?"

"Oh, come on. You're not giving up *now*. Not after the torture we put you through today." He takes the glass out of my hand and places it on the tray of a servant walking by. In turn, he grabs another full one for himself. "Besides, you really don't want her to fall for Jaccomo."

Jaccomo? "Is that the rooster's name?"

"Jaccomo Casanova, yes. I believe you've heard of the Duke of Secret Garden."

Grinding my teeth, I nod. "He's said to be a womanizer in his tale."

"Not only in the story, trust me." Lines of real worry mar Phillip's forehead. "It would be a shame if Riley fell for his charm. She won't get what she's looking for from him tonight." He snorts. "A chance at a fling at best. So to hell with your stupid pride! Go claim your girl."

My gaze shifts back to the dance floor, searching hard for flashes of pink and orange in the throng. There's a break between two songs, but the chicken doesn't give the rose a chance to escape. They're still swaying, even without music.

"Are you in need of a partner?" a soft but heavily accented voice rips me out of my murderous thoughts. "You look as if you want nothing more than to walk out onto the dance floor."

The girl is right, except that she got the reason entirely wrong. I turn and find a petite woman with caramel skin and raven black hair clinging to my arm. She's wrapped in green voile, one scarf even covering her face from the bridge of her nose downward. Next to her is another girl with basically the same face and body, only she's draped in orange voile. Twins? I'm not sure. Sisters? Definitely.

I cut a questioning glance at Phillip, but he just gives me a helpless shrug.

The eagle eyes of the girl in green are still focused on me. "I can dance with you, if you want."

Would it be very impolite to ask her to remove her hand from my arm? "No, thank you." I tuck my hands into my pockets in hopes that she'll get the hint.

Unfortunately, she doesn't understand that this is a rejection and only smiles at me. "Then why else are you looking at the dance floor with such longing?"

"Because he's nuts over the fair maiden Phillip picked for the birthday waltz," Eric jests as he joins us along with Ariel and her friend Rapunzel. Prince Thomas has his arm around the girl with hair so long one could build a rope bridge with it. Tonight, she has it braided to the back of her head…somehow. Even though I know the couple quite well, Ariel still introduces everyone, and I nod in polite greeting. My masquerade is faultless.

Apparently, the sisters in the colorful voile are named Scheherazade and Sheila. We haven't met before, but their names are well known from *One Thousand and One Nights*. I just never pictured Princess Sheila as such a clingy person.

While the women shower each other with compliments over their pretty costumes, Phillip clears his throat and, once he has my attention, he subtly nods to the dance floor. With a frown, I track his gaze and feel an avalanche of rage rushing through me as the irritating birdman heads toward us, bringing Riley along. She hurries behind him, her gaze on the ground.

"Phil…" he says, slowing down. "Nice party!" The sneer on his face hits me instead of the ball's host.

I refuse to do him the favor of showing any kind of reaction.

"Casanova," Phillip replies, a knowing, playful edge to his voice. "Taking my runaway dance partner for a walk, I see."

The chicken laughs. "Too crowded in here."

Oh, he prefers more privacy? No problem. We can head into the forest where I can stuff the feathers from his mask down his throat.

Riley chooses that moment to look up…directly at me. And all my thoughts of plucking and slaughtering are radically wiped from my mind. The only thing I want to do then is reach out for her hand and ask her to be my princess for tonight.

It doesn't escape me that her gaze switches to the girl at my side. Behind the pink mask, Riley's amber eyes glint with countless questions, but even though her lips part, she doesn't utter a single one. Maybe she would have, if Casanova didn't pull her away from us and out to the patio.

Riley slides a shy and puzzled glance at me over her shoulder before they disappear through the French doors.

I puff out a breath through gritted teeth, barely able to keep my anger in check. "Okay, that's enough." The Duke of Secret Garden just signed his death warrant.

As gently as possible in my current state, I detach my arm from Sheila's hold. "Milady, I'm sorry, but I really don't want to dance." Her disappointed eyes leave me cold.

As I stride away from the group, heading after my personal blossom, Phillip quickly sidles up to me. "Jack, what are you up to?"

Ignoring his worried tone, I forge on. "I'm doing what you told me—claiming my girl. And the chicken better not stand in my way."

One hand on my arm, he stops me and spins me to face him. "Okay, listen. I don't think Riley will even give you a chance if you splatter her dress with the blood of her escort."

"And *I* don't think you understand what's at stake here for me." I yank free of his hold and nail him with a hard glare. "If she falls for this douche, it's *The End*. I will lose everything. Our story, our friendship… *Her*."

He hesitates. "I didn't mean you should give up. Just *think* before you kill someone tonight, okay?"

From the corner of my eye, I notice a figure with an orange dress shirt walking in from the terrace. This is my chance. I plant both hands on Phillip's shoulders and sneer into his face. "I *did* think. The chicken must die."

He rolls his eyes, but he doesn't hold me back when I whirl around and start off after Casanova.

With a few fast strides, I catch up with the troublemaker and clasp the back of his shirt collar. Hauling him behind one of the columns, I press him to the marble with my elbow to this throat. The surprise in his expression is quickly replaced by annoyance. "I'm just fetching a drink for Riley. What's your damn problem, smoothy?"

His patronizing tone evokes my killer instinct. If this wasn't Phil's birthday ball, the fowl would already be bleeding out. "You're in my way," I grunt, puffing hot breath in his face.

"So what?" His provocative gaze falls to my rapier. "Are you going to skewer me to get the girl?"

"I don't need a sword to get rid of you." A dark and deadly growl rumbles from my throat.

The chicken's eyes grow a little wider in understanding. "A Wolf... I should have known." His demeaning smirk disappears, replaced by a hard, spiteful scowl. "Did you eat a prince to get his title?"

"Do *you* taste as shitty as you look with all those feathers in your hair?"

His jaw ticks. With a forceful shove against my chest, he pushes me backward a couple of steps. Bad mistake. No one puts hands on me.

My nostrils flare with fury. I leap forward, but a petite green figure moves in the way and forces me to halt my attack. Sheila is lucky I didn't knock her over. Collateral damage happens...

She holds both of her hands up to my chest, her

imploring gaze locking with mine. "Please, my lord, this isn't the right place for a fight." When she realizes that she stopped me, she takes two hesitant steps backward—into Casanova's arms. Cautiously, she tilts her head halfway to him, still keeping a watch on me while she speaks to him in a purr. "I believe earlier you promised to have a drink with me, Lord Jaccomo. So, tell me, are you a man of your word?"

His arm slides around her waist. With closed eyes, he lowers his head and nuzzles her temple, seemingly drawing in the scent of her hair. "I'm much more than that, sweethcart."

What the hell—? It's as if he's completely forgotten that I'm standing there. Or that Riley is waiting outside for him to come back with a drink. "Evidently, the legends about your fickle personality are not just rumors," I spit.

He can barely take his lustful gaze away from the Princess of the Orient. The only thing he grants me is a quick snort through his nose. "You know what, snarler? Keep the pink buttercup." He twirls a strand of Sheila's hair around his finger and strokes her cheek with his knuckles. Then he walks off with her, throwing me a final arrogant glare. "She isn't worth all this trouble."

I never wanted to kill anyone as much as I do the duke right now. But a sense of relief takes over at the realization that he lost interest in my girl.

Phil draws up to my side and chuckles. "Thanks for not drenching the feast in Casanova's blood."

My teeth grind together. "You sent her."

"Sheila? Nooo…" He lifts his hands in innocence, but he can tell his shit to someone else. His eyes glint with amusement. "She was looking for some entertainment. And the Duke of Secret Garden is renowned for his fondness for exotic women." Then he nods toward the French doors at the girl standing alone by the marble banister on the patio. "Good luck."

Laughing to myself, I shake my head. "See you later."

Riley gazes into the deep blue sky as I walk outside. It looks as if her dreams are hung up on the beauty of the night.

Sliding my hands into my pockets, I lean against a nearby tree and watch her for a moment. "They say all the stars up there are really the tears of the moon which he cried at every happy ending of a fairy tale in the world."

Her shoulders lift as she takes a deep breath before she whispers, "It is a lovely thought, isn't it?" She looks at me over her shoulder and searches my eyes. "Did the moon cry over your happy ending, too, Jacob?"

A pink rose is stuck in her hair, which wasn't there before. Casanova must have plucked it for her from the bushes growing around the patio. Only a fool wouldn't notice how smitten she is with him.

"If he cries, they are tears of laughter, I'm afraid." A chuckle escapes me because the irony isn't lost on me. "Every story needs a villain. And they never win in the end."

Apparently intrigued by my words, Riley turns around and grips the edges of the marble banister behind her hips. "So you aren't a nice guy?"

Am I? Since the beginning of fairy tales, I was told that I'm not.

I leave the shelter of the tree and walk to her side, bracing my forearms on the broad railing. My gaze runs across the garden in front of me. "I'm still trying to figure that out."

"How can you not know?" Her voice is so shy and soft, it travels through me like silk.

"Sometimes, things aren't that easy, Riley."

It feels as if her eyes bore holes into me—obviously, she's trying to figure me out. Since she's so quiet, I straighten and turn, leaning against the banister the same way she does. Head tilted, I look down at her and sigh. "Let's take your new friend Casanova for instance. If I tell you that you'll be waiting in vain for the drink he probably offered to get you because he got...*distracted* inside, would that make me a good guy or a bad one?"

Above the slim mask framing her eyes, her forehead creases. "What...?" Seconds later, the truth seems to hit. Her eyes widen, and her head snaps toward the French doors.

Riley's face pales as if a hoard of green ogres is rushing at her. Though what she actually witnesses is much worse, I'm sure. It takes three swallows for her voice to return, and it comes out flat. "She was on your arm earlier."

I cast a glance inside the ballroom just in time to find Casanova pressing a tender kiss to the princess's lips. "She was trying to get me to dance with her," I apologize that Riley had to see Sheila clinging to me.

"Why didn't you?" she sniffs. From the sound of it, she probably wishes I had. Then this terrible scene wouldn't be unfolding in front of her now. But she's missing one very important thing.

I look back at her and say, "Because it's you I wanted to dance with."

As if glued to the scene inside the ballroom where the pyramid of champagne glasses is, her gaze doesn't waver an inch. I'm not even sure she heard me. When her fingers dig hard into the banister, I stroke her bare upper arm above the glove. "Riley?" She stares straight ahead, her expression empty. "It won't get easier if you continue watching this."

A moment ticks by like we're both frozen in time. Then she slowly turns around to me. "You're right. It's just that I…"

She trails off, but I know that what she's really looking for is a way to escape the feast. All her hopes of finding this new ever after with a real prince are gone from her eyes. The excitement of this past week has disappeared. She's lost.

And once again, my heart breaks for her.

With a soft, pitiful look, I offer her my elbow, hoping we can escape together. "Would you like to take a walk through the garden?"

Heaven knows what's going on in her mind when she suddenly lifts her chin and straightens her shoulders. Her small hand slips through the crook of my arm. Taking this as her answer, I start walking, but Riley holds me back and calls, "Wait!" With an angry frown, she tears the pink rose from her hair and smacks it so hard on the railing that a couple of the petals scatter. Then she beams at me with all the pride I'm used to from the woods. "Okay, now we can go."

Damn. My admiration for this girl grows with every new day. One moment, it seems like she's lost her spirit. And the next, it rolls back into town with double force. It's impossible to keep my smirk in check.

I almost have to shake myself to remember that I'm just staring at her. Her hand caught tightly between my arm and my side, we start off along the path leading away from the patio and out into the seven acres of green that make up the castle's gardens. As if walking on shards of glass, the pebbles crunch beneath our steps. For a long time, it's the only sound I hear, the noise from the feast having faded a while ago.

Even though Riley clings to my arm, a sideways glance at her face reveals that she's disappeared into a world of her own and is likely having quite the animated dialog with herself. Her mouth shifts from one side to the other, and her eyebrows rise and fall. Under the mask, her snub nose wrinkles, and she sniffs with determination.

The longer I watch her, the bigger my smile grows.

"It's amazing, the multitude of emotions your face can shift through in less than two minutes."

Startled out of her private conversation, she swirls around to me. A moment passes. The intenseness almost swipes me off my feet. Then she cracks a grin and drops the most inept curtsey of all time. "Glad I could entertain you, my lord."

A laugh rattles in my chest. "You never cease to, Riley."

Instantly, her gaze takes on a suspicious note. "You've only known me for an hour."

Oh, dear girl, how wrong you are. I press her hand tighter to my side. "Really? Felt like at least a week to me." Or an eternity…

The main party may take place in the castle, but the spell of the feast definitely carries out here, too. While the guys had fun turning me into a prince this afternoon, Rory made sure to have the staff dig out every piece of décor there was and then used it to change the garden into a fairy tale of its own.

Lanterns hang like will-o'-the-wisps from the trees. Every twenty feet, petite wooden frames arch across the path, and Riley inhales deeply as we stroll through the tunnel. Tendrils of roses decorate them like the columns in the ballroom. They're always in bloom in this garden because the Timeless Brook runs across this piece of land. The enchanted water that constantly flows backward holds lots of mystical properties, the most striking one: to keep everyone and everything in an unchanging state. Who knows what Fairyland and its inhabitants would look like today if we didn't have this spring of magic constantly nourishing us.

The pebbled path ends near a stone bridge leading across the little river. Hercules and his wife stroll toward us, and we all exchange polite nods in greeting as we pass each other, even though it looks as if they don't recognize Riley or me.

On the other side of the river, the pebbled walkway continues toward the duck pond. It's a basin nurtured from the Timeless Brook and surrounded by a stone wall no higher than my hip. A fountain of ivory towers in the middle, and from seven spouts, thin streams of water drip down like liquid silver.

A duck family sleeps peacefully in the grass nearby as we approach. While Riley stops by the wall and gazes at the fountain, the drake lifts his head, maybe stirred by the dangerous aura of a Wolf penetrating the night. My placating smile does little to appease him, and he keeps nailing me with his beady eye. I almost expect him to flutter up and attack me to protect his mate and five ducklings. To show that his family isn't in any danger of getting eaten, I lower my gaze to the water in front of me and stir it with my finger, inconspicuously watching the waterfowl from the corner of my eye. Eventually, he lowers his head back into his wing and closes his eyes again.

Riley rubs her arms and pulls my attention back to

her.

"Are you cold? Would you like my jacket?" I fumble with the top button to open it.

"No, thank you, I'm fine. It's a lovely night." When she smiles, my hands sink back down. Still, a slightly worried look lingers in her eyes, and she hitches up her skirt from the ground as if ready to walk again. "But maybe we should go back. I don't want to keep you away from the feast for too long."

Keep me away? Well, that's hardly what she's doing. "Don't worry about it." Hopefully, my smile reassures her more than it did the drake earlier. "Actually, I didn't want to come to this ball at all."

Her forehead creases in wonder. "Why not?"

"Mostly because of the company." And asshole Casanova proved my point. Turning around, I hoist myself up to sit on the wall ledge overlooking the pond. "Crowded places make me nervous. Frankly, I'm not a big fan of royal show-offs."

That sure raises her curiosity. Her head tilts, and her eyes narrow as she scrutinizes me on the way over to a maple tree as if afraid I'd end in smoke if she lets me out of sight even for a second. Her hands go behind her back as a buffer as she leans against the rough trunk. "Then why did you come?"

For you, honeydrop.

"I'm here because of a friend," I reveal half of the truth with a nonchalant shrug. "And of course, it's Phillip's birthday."

"Right. Your cousin," she murmurs as if she completely forgot. Then a provocative gleam enters her gaze. "But the company clinging to your arm earlier didn't look too bad."

I wrinkle my nose. "Scheherazade and her sister Sheila are just additional proof why I don't like princesses around me. They hang on to me. No doubt, some of them are really funny and nice." Aurora and the Mermaid are lovely princesses. "But mostly, there's something important missing from those girls, and they usually can't hold my attention for longer than five minutes."

"And what is that…something important?" Shards of bark fall to the ground around her dress, and I wonder if she's peeling the husk off the tree for some reason. Is she nervous?

"I don't know." My gaze lowers briefly. If I had to take a random guess, it's just everything that forms *her*. Her love of adventure, her kind spirit, the fact that she doesn't mind jumping into puddles and walking the rest of the way with dirty boots. I love how she never smothers her laughter behind her hand, and that she doesn't wait to answer a question until she's swallowed a bite of food in her mouth. She lives every single minute as if it's a sacred present. Riley is a force of nature. One that swipes you off your feet when it rolls over you.

One day, I hope I can tell her all of this, but now is not the right time. So I look at her again and sum it up. "A certain spark maybe."

She takes a long moment to think on that, and the intensity of our locked gazes begins to sizzle. Perhaps she even understands what I just tried to tell her. At least, she gives me the feeling that she does. Finally, as if testing a theory, she whispers, "If you detest princesses so much, then why did you want to dance with me?"

Oh yes, she's definitely on the right track. I chuckle with fire in my eyes. "You aren't a princess, Riley."

Her gasp echoes in the silent night. "How can you say that?"

"Because you're different."

Her mouth drops open but, this time, no words come out. I slide off the stone wall and draw closer, eyes fixed on her. The deep red crown of the tree with its overhanging branches cuts off the moonlight. Riley watches my every step, her body tensing, her eyes growing wider.

"Do you want to know what really made me walk up to you in the hallway?" I drawl as I come to a stop right in front of her and press my palm on the trunk next to her head. Her chest lifts with fast breaths. "Any other girl in such a striking dress wouldn't have waited a second to walk down the stairs," I whisper, leaning even closer. "She would have been dying to show off to all the people in the hall." My hand slips around her hip to the small of her back, bringing us into a really intimate position. "But you hesitated. I saw how nervous you were—how you held on to the curtains for support. You looked intimidated by the thought of facing the ball."

Riley blinks a few times, her nervousness tangible when she remains quiet. I don't want to make her feel uncomfortable, even though I'm not entirely sure that it's discomfort she feels at my touch. I tilt my head, my voice softening. "Am I wrong?"

An eternity passes while a multitude of emotions race across her face. Finally, she clears her throat. "No, you're right. I'm not a princess." She sounds as if it cost her all the effort in the world to tell me the truth. "I don't belong here. It was a stupid idea to come in the first place."

"Where *do* you belong?" She can certainly feel the breath of my whisper on her skin. A mere inch separates our lips now, a space hardly allowed to be called a distance.

Riley swallows. And then she breaks away from me before I can even react. As if in a panic from what could happen, she rushes away but stops after a few steps and spins back to me. With more than ten feet between us now, it appears easier for her to answer my question. "In the woods. It's the only place I've ever known as home."

Coping with her fidgeting, I follow her with a deliberate gait. She takes one step back for each of mine forward. Riley's shyness coaxes my smile, which in turn makes her stop abruptly. Good. Slowly, I close the distance until I can take her hands in mine. Now, I'm the one walking backward. I tug her with me and lean against the stone wall of the duck pond once more. "You seem like you have an interesting story to tell." Her petite hands tremble a little in mine as I make her stand right in front of me. The space between my spread legs is jammed with her puffy skirt. "What's your tale, Riley?"

"There's not much to tell, really." Her bashful gaze lowers to our joined hands. "I just spend a lot of time in the forest."

I try to recapture her gaze, but she doesn't let me, so I ask in a gentle tone, "What do you do there?"

Her shoulders lift in a helpless shrug. "Talk to someone and try to save my family from an attack."

Because she still refuses to look at me, I let go of her hand and gently lift her chin with my knuckle. My fingers linger lightly against the crook of her neck. "Do you get a happy ending?"

"I do." She nods and then hesitates. "But not the way I wish."

"What way would that be?"

Her lips press into a thin line. Was that a step too far? Even though we've spent years and years together in our tale, tonight, I'm a stranger to her. I'm close to apologizing for my bold question when the quiet truth slips from her lips. "I never get kissed."

A bolt of longing zaps through me. *You have no idea how much I would love to change that right now.* I brush my thumb along her jawline, my gaze zeroing in on her heart-shaped mouth. "What a shame…and a waste."

The next instant, images of us under the tree and her escaping from me when I got too close flash before me. I don't want to scare her away again, so I drop my hands and brace them on either side of my hips on the stone barrier, coughing a little to find my voice again. "Isn't there a guy in your story?"

"Oh, sure there is." The grin that splits her face is a surprise. Does that always happen when she thinks about me?

I catch her with a playful look. "So he's an idiot?" Yes, I definitely am for not kissing her even once in all this time.

Riley gives me a little pony snicker. "No. Jack isn't an idiot. He's smart and funny." Then her expression suddenly changes as she goes quiet for a second. In a much softer tone, she adds, "And caring… In fact, he's one of the best men I know."

My chin drops. *Damnit, think of your role, Jack!* I have to inwardly shake myself out of this stupor and resist pulling her into my arms for a tender embrace. With forced lightness, I joke, "Sounds as if you like this guy a lot. Do I have a rival?"

"A rival?" Riley laughs, backing away a step and eyeing me sideways. "Why, Jacob? Are you fighting for my heart?"

She pretends to be sassy. But I think, in truth, she's afraid of the answer. Because what if I say yes? Would she be able to handle it? I bet that's what she's wondering right now.

The Wolf inside me awakens and starts clawing at me, insisting that it's time to stop playing the well-mannered prince and just grab what we both want. And he's damn right. I push away from the stone wall and prowl toward Red Riding Hood, licking my lips.

She certainly noticed that the game just upped a level because she timidly draws back until the same maple tree stops her again. I close the distance and cup her cheeks with both hands, not allowing her gaze to escape me this time. Hitched breaths whiz through her parted mouth, and her eyes sparkle like frightened little stars. I run my thumb over her bottom lip, dip my head down a little, and whisper, "Fighting for your heart, I am. Didn't you notice that yet?"

Anticipation has my heart in a tight grip. It feels as if it took forever and a week to come here. I inhale deeply and then press a gentle kiss to her lips. It's only the softest touch of innocence. And it feels amazing—like with this sensitive brush alone, Riley just launched a tune of pure sweetness inside my mind.

I let my lips dance with hers to the song until she opens her mouth for me. My tongue sweeps inside and slides against hers with tender slowness. The honor of being her very first kiss floods me, causing the skin at the back of my neck to bristle. *Oh, honeydrop, you can't even begin to understand...*

Suddenly, a strange feeling rolls through me, a longing to kiss her deeper but not under the covers of a mask anymore. I want her to truly see me when she responds to my caress. For her to look into my eyes and recognize Jack, not someone who doesn't exist.

Ending the kiss is one of the toughest battles I have ever fought because Riley tastes absolutely wonderful. We should be doing this every day. For hours. But not here. Not now. I catch her upper lip between mine for one last, endearing touch. Then I inch away.

Moments later, Riley slowly blinks her eyes open, like she's emerging from a dream. The amber in her irises shines as if the orbs are burning in the moonlight. I brush my fingertips from her neck down over her shoulders and along her gloved arms until we can lace our fingers. Her face irradiates as she smiles at me and sighs.

A strange breeze suddenly wafts over us, causing her dress and several escaped locks from her updo style to fly in the wind. The ground trembles beneath my feet ever so slightly, as if the briefest shiver just raced through Fairyland. An ice-cold shudder runs through me, too. It feels like something…cracked. And there's only one thought in my mind.

Our story.

Everybody here in the world of fairy tales knows of this power. The force that alone can bring change. Riley kept talking about it all week. *The kiss of true love.*

But is that really what happened? After all, she doesn't know who I am. In her eyes, I'm Prince Jacob of the Snow Plains. A complete stranger—someone who doesn't even exist, for Grimm's sake. We've only spent two hours together at this ball. It's way too quick to fall in love with someone and break our tale. Right?

My stomach churns. Holy Prince and the Pauper, was it a mistake to come here as a royal?

A moment later, the wind dissipates, and the quaking stops. Only the odd feeling as if something has changed remains within me. The tiny hairs on the back of my neck stand on end.

Riley flexes her fingers between mine, her gaze turning worried as she searches my face. I realize that I must have been squashing her hands given how tightly I was gripping them. Shaking my head, I release her and clear my throat. Perhaps I'm reading the situation completely wrong, and there's nothing going on to put our tale in danger. Hopefully…

She opens her mouth, but instead of saying anything, all color drains from her cheeks, and her eyes widen with a whole different kind of shock.

Damn, is the drake about to attack? Instinctively, my head snaps around, but the duck family still sleeps peacefully in the grass. I turn back to Riley. "Is everything okay?"

"Yes, everything's perfect," she tells me quickly.

I'm pretty sure it's a lie because the smile she gives me is all but a facial cramp. Just when her mien starts to soften, another zap of shock seems to hit her. She hooks her hand to my arm and pulls me away from the shelter of the tree. Under her forcefully calm expression, there is blank panic. "Can we walk a bit?"

My narrow-eyed gaze skates from left to right. I can't

hear or see anything that would put us in acute danger. Unless—

Oh, fuck. She felt the crack, too, and now she's freaking out.

But is that a good sign or a bad one? By Grimm's quill, I don't know! If she's falling in love with a stranger who doesn't exist, I'm screwed. If, however, she just realized that Prince Jacob is not her type and that she's really into Jack Wolf, things might take a lucky turn for me, after all.

Walking is a good idea. It gives me time to think. "Sure," I murmur, bending my arm and shoving the other hand into my pocket as we amble off.

Riley walks pretty fast. This is not a cozy stroll, and thinking is impossible. She keeps looking over her shoulder. Soon, it feels as if we're actually on the run from something. Bees, ducks, a void that eats storyless characters…who the hell knows.

More and more, I come to the conclusion that my disguise was the most stupid idea I could have ever come up with. How do I get out of this charade now? I didn't put much thought into the ending of my plan when we set it all up. If Riley truly falls in love with Jacob, she'll hate me for lying to her when she hears the truth.

And if she realizes that she's in love with Jack in truth, she'll kill me twice over for fooling her.

Either way, I'm dead. Fantastic.

Only when we reach the stone bridge over the

Timeless Brook again does her grip on my arm loosen a little, and her steps slow. I try to capture her gaze every time she casts a glance behind us, but she doesn't give me a chance. As if she's afraid I'll be able to read something in her eyes that's supposed to be a secret. Funny, since I'm the imposter here.

Then again, maybe she figured me out already?

I deliberately slow us down even more as we walk across the bridge. "Riley, did I do something wrong?" My voice is soft yet insistent. Let's hear what she says before I come out with the truth.

She keeps her attention focused on the ground. "No. No, you didn't. That was...what you did..." Her stammering breaks off as she finally lifts her head and her eyes fill with longing. "It was beautiful."

The kiss? My heart melts a little because I thought so, too. So she actually has no clue about the truth yet. "Then why are you being so evasive now?"

"I'm not. I just..." Her apologetic look is confusing me all to hell. Waiting for her to continue, I lift my brows in expectation. In the next moment, she downright stiffens beside me, and her face goes blank once more.

"You...what?" I urge her to speak, but she ignores me and tries to escape.

"Nothing. We should go back to the feast."

Oh no, Red Riding Hood, we aren't going anywhere right now. I grab her wrist. "Stop!" Riley knocks against my chest as I haul her back, and a surprised gasp leaves her.

Steadying her with a grip on her arms, I nail her with a scowl. "What's wrong?"

Her mouth drops open.

Okay, so maybe that was a little harsh. I try it again, this time much softer. "If the kiss was a mistake, then tell me... Don't just run away."

"I'm so sorry, but it's late. I need to leave!" She tugs at her hand. When I refuse to let her escape, her face scrunches in desperation. "Please, Prince Jacob, you must let me go. I can't stay here."

"Only for a few more minutes, I beg you." We really need to talk this out.

Since she can't free her hand from my firm grip, she begins to fidget and whine. What in the world is up with her? Did the call of the story set in again, after all? I wouldn't notice thanks to Dr. Jekyll's elixir, but if she's feeling the pull, she should just say so.

Torn by her obvious misery, I finally let go of her hand. If she wants away from me so badly, who am I to stop her?

As soon as she's free, Riley hitches up her skirt, about to dash off. Then suddenly, my own despair is mirrored in her eyes, and she whimpers, "I don't want to go. Really. I wish I could stay the entire night out here in the garden with you, but I can't."

Just when I think that perhaps she really does want to stay with me, she speeds off the bridge. *Fail, Jack!*

"I need to tell you something," I call after her. Maybe

the truth can set it all right. "It's important!"

Instantly, she whips around and dashes toward me again. Wow, that was fast. A bolt of hope zooms through me that I finally found the right argument to make her stay, and my face lifts with relief.

Riley stops in front of me, her gaze still tortured. I reach out for her hand…

And she goes *poof!*

I blink at the empty spot. "Riley?"

Nothing. There's nothing left of her. Not even a hint of smoke.

Panic floods me as I twist on the spot, scanning for her everywhere. *"Riley?"*

The hoot of an owl is the only reply, but that is certainly not her. With my heart now battering violently in my chest, I run to the stone ledge of the bridge and lean over. "Riley, where the hell are you?"

The Timeless Brook flows in its ever-calm way backward in the riverbed. There isn't a single disturbance to show that a girl dropped into the water two seconds ago.

Petrified, I spin around, raking my hands through my powdered hair. My gaze zooms all over the place, only to find that I'm utterly alone in the garden. Riley has literally vanished into thin air. My blood runs cold.

Good Grimm, I killed her.

Chapter 5

I click my heels together three times…and suddenly, I fall. There's nothing but wind and a deep blue night sky around me. The stone bridge over the Timeless Brook is gone. The water, too. Heck, the entire castle and its gardens have disappeared.

I scream my lungs out.

For seconds on end, I drop into nothingness. And then, there's a haystack.

"*Aaaaah*—whoop!" Butt-first, I land on the grassy cushion—naked. Thankfully, I still have on my red panties

77

and Dorothy's ruby slippers. When the first shock fades, and I can breathe again, I look around in the moonlit night. Flat landscapes, a forest in the distance, and a farm to my right. "Ah, Kansas."

After battling my way down from the stack, I brush some straw out of my hair and, covering my breasts with my arms, sneak over to Aunt Em's house. It's a minute past midnight—I know, because Cindy's darn dress disappeared at the twelfth strike of the grandfather clock, which the Fairy Godmother kept pointing at—and I don't want to wake anyone up in this part of Fairyland. Especially not when all my clothes are gone. I would be the next flashing headline in *The Character Magazine. Naked thief breaks into Dorothy Gale's home.*

In front of the porch, I take off the shoes and tiptoe up the stairs. The wooden planks creak under my feet. Dang, I cringe at every single step. Right outside the door, I stoop and carefully put the slippers down. In that very instant, pain explodes in my head. I'm thrown backward to the floor, and the world around me switches off.

∗

A wet tongue licking my face wakes me.

"Ugh!" Eyes squeezed tightly, I shove at a furry snout. "Jack. Is that you? Stop it."

If it really is him, he shrank to a size where he can stand on my chest.

"Toto! Get down!" the command of a girl rings out, followed by the click of a closing door.

When the face-licking stops and the furball jumps off me, I force my eyes open. Daylight shrivels them to raisins. Shit, my head hurts.

Face now covered by my arms, I whine. "Where am I?"

"In Kansas." The mattress dips beside me as the girl lowers. She lifts my arms away and dabs my forehead with a wet cloth. "In my room at Aunt Em's house."

Cautiously, I blink my eyes open again. This time, I don't feel like Count Dracula in the sun. Still, I'm completely out of place here. "And why am I lying in your bed?"

Dorothy Gale smiles down at me. Two braids of auburn hair frame her face, and she's wearing the only outfit I've ever seen her in—a light blue gingham dress, and a white blouse with short, puffy sleeves. "Because you were unconscious for a while."

When she grimaces, she makes me believe that it's not a very nice story. Shivers of unease run through my body. "Did the Wicked Witch of the West get me?"

"No." She draws a stream of air in between her teeth. "The door."

"Ah…" Well, that makes absolutely no sense.

She bends down to lift a whimpering Toto onto her lap. When she starts rubbing behind his ear, and he leans his head happily into her hand, the image looks strangely familiar. "A short while ago, my ruby slippers vanished," she explains. "My first thought was that the green shrew came and took them." Clutching the tiny dog under her arm, Dorothy stands and crosses to the desk by the wall to open the window above it. The smell of hay and cows wafts into the small but cozy room. "Around midnight, I heard a noise outside and ran, hoping to catch the witch. When I stormed out through the door, I obviously hit you on the head." She turns around and leans against the edge of the desk, wrinkling her nose as she presses Toto to her chest. "It looked like you were trying to get through the cat flap."

Holy tornado from Oz…was I?

"Do you remember why you were crouched outside the door? Or why you came here so late at night anyway?"

"No." Eyes narrowed in confusion, I scoot up against the headboard into a seated position, pulling the blanket with me. The white-and-blue-striped nightgown I'm wearing is definitely not mine, so I guess I didn't come here for a sleepover.

"What's the last thing you do remember?"

Thinking hard, I try to recall what I did yesterday. I woke up, and Jack was gone. He left a note on my kitchen table. Then I went into the forest to check my prince trap and found Sleepy in it. After that, things fog up quite a bit. I rub my forehead. "It could be that a woman in a purple dressing gown with hair curlers tried to break into my house."

"Did she steal your clothes?" Dorothy demands, head

tilted. "Because you came here almost naked."

I don't know her definition of *almost*, but her quizzical look is enough to drive flames of embarrassment to my cheeks. I lower my gaze. "Thanks for the nightie."

Still, I don't believe I left my house without clothes on. In fact, I have a feeling that I was wearing something beautiful. "Hey, wait!" Didn't I dig out my mother's old gown from the chest under my bed?

Of course, I did! As a wave of excitement rushes through me, I sit up straighter. "I dressed up for a ball in Aurora's castle last night. It was Phillip's birthday! Only…" Realization deadens my voice. "The gown caught on fire, and a mud puddle saved me from burning. I don't think I wore the rag to the feast." Did I go to the masked ball at all? And how does the lady with the yellow crocs fit in?

Dorothy comes closer again. She puts the cairn terrier in my lap and fills a glass with water from a jar on the nightstand, which she then offers to me. I take a sip as she sits down. "The only thing you had on was your panties. Not even a bra, Riley." Her tone, so reproachful, doesn't match her cramping cheeks. She's obviously biting back a giggle.

Dorothy and I hang out in the woods together occasionally, trying to train her dog to do new tricks. Other times, we meet at the library in Grimmwich. We know each other well and can chat for ages, even after not getting together for a long time. But that *doesn't* entitle either of us to see the other naked. Dang, I wouldn't even want Jack to get a close-up of my boobs.

Instinctively, I wrap my arms tightly across my chest over the covers and grimace. "Maybe I was in a hurry when I left the house…"

"To get to the ball? I heard it was for royals only."

Royals… Absently, I rake my fingers through Toto's scrubby fur. "Right, it was. I got a special invitation because I was looking for a prince."

Her eyes widen with interest. "What do you need a prince for?"

"Ugh, long story…"

Dorothy tugs her feet under her bottom, pulls the blue dress over her knees, and gets comfortable. "I've got nothing to do." A grin splits her face. "Shoot."

Very well. I start at the beginning, the meeting with the princesses last weekend, and fill Dorothy in on my plans to catch a royal and write my own love story. "The prince trap and every attempt before that were major failures. Phillip's celebration was my last resort. But no matter how hard I try, I can't blow away the fog that's misting the events of the actual ball night."

"Did the Wolf get an invitation, too?"

"I wanted Jack to come with me, but he said no. He wasn't even in town yesterday."

She fixes me with a stoic look. "The ball was on Friday."

"Yes…which was yesterday." A queasy feeling churns my stomach. "Right?"

Her tongue darts out to wet her lips and, once again, she draws in a breath through her front teeth. "Maybe I should have mentioned it before… It's Sunday afternoon. Apart from a few half-awake moments, you've slept through two days."

"By all good fairy tales, Dorothy!" I jump out of bed, making little Toto fly aside with the blanket. "How hard did you hit me on the head?"

"Hey, I was in a hurry to catch the shoe thief," she defends herself, hands lifted. Then she puts them down as her dog climbs back onto her lap. "Speaking of, where did you find them?"

My naked toes curl against the wooden floor. "Find what?"

"My ruby slippers. They were lying next to your sprawled, unconscious body."

My brows tip into a frown. "I had your ruby slippers?" The next instant, my eyes pop wide as everything flashes in fast-forward before me. "I had your ruby slippers! Of course!" I used them to escape from Prince Jacob. If I hadn't, he would've gotten an exclusive look at my boobs instead of my friend.

Hyped by the flood of beautiful memories, I dash back to the bed and snatch Toto out of Dorothy's hands. Kissing him on the head in sheer delight, I dance with him through the room, telling Dorothy everything—from the Fairy Godmother's visit, to why I wasn't allowed to wear Cindy's glass slippers, and all about the ride on the robin horse. Her brows draw together at the part where Jaccomo dumped me for the princess of the Orient, but relax when I relay how Jacob took me for a stroll through the garden.

"Oh, he kissed me in the moonlight," I gush, shoulders raised, and my eyes dreamily shut against the warm afternoon sun. "You can't imagine how beautiful it was." With a zestful swing of my arms, Toto flies out through the open window.

"Riley!" Dorothy squeals, half laughing, half in shock as she skips from the bed and rushes to the desk, bracing her hands on it to scan outside. The gray terrier has already taken off after a goose. He regularly gets caught in a tornado—he's used to flying.

When she whips back around to face me, her eyes sparkle with amusement. "Are you actually in love?"

"I think I am." In the middle of a swirl, I stop dead, and my smile falls. "Goodness me, I need to go back to the castle! Jacob came down from the Snow Plains." In a panic, I dash to the door. "I hope he's still there!"

"Red Riding Hood…!" Dorothy's challenging call stops me. She comes over, folds her arms, and lifts her brows. "You want to meet your prince in a nightgown?"

I look down at the striped garment hanging on me with my bare feet peeping out. "Oh."

"Come on, you muddlehead." Giggling, she loops her hand through mine and pulls me to the country-style wardrobe. As she opens the door with flowers carved into the fair wood, the monstrosity reveals a wide selection of…blue gingham dresses and white blouses.

That's exactly why we need a prince with a castle. Duh!

I wiggle myself into one of her outfits while Dorothy tries to sway me into borrowing her boots, too. "No thanks, I've had enough of borrowed shoes this week." My face scrunches as we hug goodbye. "Besides, I don't mind walking barefoot."

She crosses her fingers and sees me off at the door. Then she calls after me, "Let me know if he asks you to marry him!"

In a twirl, I give her a grin and two thumbs up. Then I flitter through the forest back to Castle Grove. Jacob is Phillip's cousin. With some luck, he stayed for a while.

All the excitement makes me thirsty. There's a spot near the mill that's good for drinking from the Timeless Brook, so I drop to my knees and cup a few draughts with my hands. "Wuh!" a shriek escapes me as I catch a glimpse of myself in the water's surface. My locks, still wound and fastened to my head, stick out in every possible direction. I've lain this swept-up hairdo to death in Dorothy's bed.

For endless minutes, I pull out every single hairpin and drop them into the skirt pocket. Jacob would get the shock of his life if he saw the girl he kissed looking like a scarecrow. Raking my fingers through my long strands will hopefully give them a nice flow again. Not perfect, but pretty enough to meet a prince.

I run the rest of the way. Every minute counts because

Jacob could be getting ready to go home. Out of breath as I reach the bridge across the moat, I slow down and use the final few steps to calm myself. Only when my panting ceases do I use the brass doorknob to sound out three echoing knocks.

Rory's servant Edgar opens the door. His face lights up. He always smiles when he sees me, mostly because I usually bring greetings from my granny. But not today. "Miss Red Riding Hood, what a pleasure to see you! You had the prince and princess seriously worried, my child."

"Did I?" I clasp my fingers together. "Are they home perhaps?"

Behind the butler, Phillip walks into the hall through the French doors that lead out to the stables. "Riley?" He rushes forward with gleaming eyes. Edgar slides out of the way just in time. If he hadn't, Phillip would have run him over in his attempt to sweep me up into an unexpected embrace. "Thank Grimm, you're alive!"

My face scrunches in confusion as the air squeezes out of my lungs. My gaze darts nervously from side to side. "Uh, yeah…" Dorothy knocked out my lights, she didn't kill me.

"Everyone was looking for you! Where have you been?" He puts me down on my feet and drags me inside, leaving Edgar to close the door. The heels of his riding boots clack on the stone floor. "We were scared as hell when you disappeared from the feast. Jac…*cob* said you popped into thin air and vanished." With a tight grip on my elbows as if afraid I might disappear again, he fixes me with a demanding stare. "What happened?"

"There was a problem with the dress. I had to get it…um…fixed."

"Phillip? Is that Riley? Did you find her?"

At Rory's voice behind me, I zoom around and find her hobbling out of the kitchen, the same anxiety burning in her look as her husband had before.

"Edgar just let her in," Phillip tells her as he shrugs out of his riding jacket and tosses it aside.

Balancing on her crutches, Aurora makes her way toward us, and I wrap my arms around her.

"It's so good to see you," she squeals. "Just where have you been? Cindy kept checking the magical shrine—said maybe you got caught in the dress when it returned. But the gown came back alone. We searched the entire garden for you. And the guys were hunting the town and forest nonstop the past two days."

Oh. Who could have guessed my disappearance would cause such an uproar? "I lost track of time at the feast." Bashfully, I rub my neck. "And then I had to run because I didn't want to stand naked before Prince Jacob. Or any other guest, for that matter."

"Jacob said you just disappeared," Rory repeats Phillip's words from earlier with a quizzical expression and then throws her hands in the air. "Like…*poof.*"

My face tips into a sheepish grin. "I had Dorothy's shoes."

Both of them look at me as if the horn of a unicorn just shot from my forehead.

For better understanding, I click my bare heels together. "Clack, clack, clack…?"

The next second, they throw each other a glance and then break into laughter. "Did the shoes sweep you off to Oz?" Aurora asks.

"No. Kansas. But I had a little run-in with a door and spent the past two days in Dorothy's bed with a mild concussion."

"Ow." She crinkles her nose in real sympathy. "Sounds painful."

"Don't worry, it's all good now." I throw a look around the palace and sadly find that everything is back to normal. No decorations on the walls or the stairwell, no candles, and no rose petals on the floor anymore. "Have all the guests left?"

"The ball ended in the early morning hours, and everyone went home afterward."

My gaze skates to Phillip, my voice turning into a mouse tweep. "Jacob, too?"

He hesitates a second before he nods.

Dang! Like a sack of flour, my heart drops to the ground. "What a shame."

"Yes, he said he couldn't leave his kingdom alone for too long. But you know what?" Grinning, Rory hands me one of the crutches and hooks her free hand to my arm. Using me as her living cane, she hobbles as we walk to the parlor. "Before he left, he told me that he totally fell in love with you. Apparently, he's never met a girl as sweet as you before."

And just like that, my heart grows wings again. A blissful warmth surges to my cheeks as I turn to Phillip and check for his opinion. After all, he should know his cousin best, right? We share a look, and the impish arch of his eyebrows sparks my wide smile.

Aurora giggles, squeezing my arm. "It wouldn't surprise me if he wants to marry you."

A cozy feeling spreads inside me, and then a sudden thought comes to my mind. I help her onto a yellow upholstered chair and take the second crutch from her. "Maybe I can visit the Snow Plains and meet Prince Jacob there."

"Ooh, that's a genius idea!" she claps her hands in elation. "He'll be so happy to see you." Her beaming gaze zooms to her husband. "Right, honey?"

However, Phillip doesn't seem to share her enthusiasm. In fact, he looks as if he's just been mauled by Simba's entire pride. *"Whaaat…?"*

"Well, he could be Riley's new happy ending. She just needs to go find him."

His gulp echoes in the room as his eyes plead with me. "Could you talk to Jack about this first?"

"No, he isn't in town, remember?" And I don't want to waste another minute. The past two days in Dorothy's house have already cost me too much.

"Oh, he *is* back. And he's been out of his mind with worry ever since he heard about your disappearance." Placing his hands on my shoulders, he moves me backward until I slump onto a cushioned sofa. "Before you do anything reckless, you should go see him."

"There's no time for that." Pressing the crutches tighter to my chest, I shake my head. "What if Jacob finds another princess in the meantime? I need to leave as soon as possible."

"She's right, honey," Aurora supports me and then beams at me again. "What's the fastest way up into the North?"

"I don't know. Ship?"

"Ooh, I think Jacob said he came with a ship, too." Thrilled, she kneads her pink skirt with her fingers. "The journey should only take a day, right, Phillip?"

Her husband sinks onto the chair across from me. All of a sudden, he looks a bit pale. I frown. "Are you sick?"

He slumps deeper and rubs his hands over his face. "*Pleeease!* Talk to Jack."

What the heck—boys and their friendships. "Okay…" Rolling my eyes, I get to my feet and push the crutches into Phillip's hands. "I'll try to get ahold of him before I leave." If Jack is back from wherever he ran off to on Thursday night, it would be nice to see him again anyway.

I bend down to hug Rory where she sits on the chair. "I'll be back soon."

"Take care." She kisses me on the cheek and gives me

an approving nod. "I'll send Edgar out with telegrams to the girls to let them know you're all right."

Her husband passes the crutches back to her and walks me to the front door. "You *are* going to talk to Jack first, right? Promise me," he demands as he lets me out into the sunny afternoon.

A sigh escapes me. "Promise." I draw an *X* over my heart and mentally add: *if he's home when I get there.*

Unfortunately, the detour to Grimmwich and to Jack's apartment above Geppetto's workshop is a big waste of time. Jack isn't home. He might be sitting in the pub, but that's a place I damn sure won't step a foot into.

A cloud of sadness envelops me. I really would have loved to see him, maybe even ask him to come with me on the journey. Last week with him was fun, and he was quite a big help with the prince trap. But I can't wait too much longer, not when my ever after is on the line.

Since the harbor isn't far from here, I take a chance and run down to book the earliest cruise to the North. A man with an eye patch and a wooden leg sits on a barrel at the Limping River Wharf, drinking from a bottle of rum. Drops of the liquor glisten in his shaggy beard.

I approach him with a wary smile. "Hello, sir. I need to go to the Snow Plains to meet a prince. We fell in love at a ball Friday night, and I believe he might want to marry me. Would you be able to tell me which ship is leaving for the North today?"

Bottle in hand, he points at a mighty craft with the

name *Flying Dutchman* painted on its black hull.

"Well, thank you very much." After a polite nod, I turn and start off toward the ghost ship. Surely someone on board can tell me at what time they sail.

The man burps behind me. "Ye better run, lass, 'cause it's about to leave."

"What?" I whirl back to the pirate. "That's far too soon! I have to go home and pack my things. I don't even have money on me to pay for the cruise." And I can hardly confront Prince Jacob in the Marble Mountains with bare feet, looking so unkempt. "When does the next ship set sail?"

"There is no next ship." He spits brown goo onto the ground. "Ye sail with the *Dutchman* or not at all."

My shoulders drop. "But…" Helplessly, I spin on the spot and then point at the *Jolly Roger* cozily bobbing in the waves a little father off. "What about that one?"

"Hook doesn't sail to the North. If ye have a prince in Neverland, ye can go with the captain." The freebooter toasts me with his bottle and takes another large swig.

A deep sigh escapes me as I watch the men aboard the *Flying Dutchman* hoist the heavy anchor, pulling in one thick chain link at a time.

"Excuse me, lassie." The drunken pirate gets up and hands me the empty bottle. He sniffs, spits more nasty stuff onto the ground, and wipes his mouth with the back of his dirty paw. "Gotta catch me ride."

While he limps off to the ship that I should be on

board, all I can do is stare at it with a breaking heart. Coaches don't go to the rocky North of Fairyland, so a ship was my best bet. I hug the stinking bottle to my chest. Getting to Prince Jacob has turned into a harder challenge than expected. But I won't give up.

As the sun makes its descent in the west, I toss the rum bottle away and start back for home. Maybe I'll come up with another idea once I'm out of Dorothy's dress and wrapped in my pretty red cloak again. Who can think clearly in so much blue and white anyway? Also, the heat out here is getting to my head, and I'm longing for the cooler woods.

At the crossroads in the Wood of 1000 Dawns where Jack usually waits for me, a strange melancholy grips me. I stop and gently stroke the signpost. It's only been a week, but it feels like I haven't been Red Riding Hood for years. How is it for Jack? Does he miss playing our tale?

Do I?

If Prince Jacob does marry me, I may never come back here. He'll probably want me to live in his castle in the Snow Plains so we can start our story. And Jack...? Will we write letters and still be friends? After seeing each other every single day for as long as we've both lived, this feels extremely odd.

Shaking off the emotion, I take the turn toward Glitter Hollow. My naked toes curl deeper into the cool soil with every step. Boy, it's good to be home. Breathing deeply, I replay the lovely evening with Jacob in my mind.

The dance, the walk, the kiss… A big smile settles on my lips, and I even start humming the tune from my and Jack's story.

As I come to the mighty oak tree close to my hut, a round of robins rises from it and flies in a perfect circle above my head. What, is the Fairy Godmother coming back to scold me for the fiasco at the ball? I snicker.

But soon, all sounds die in my throat as my cozy little cottage appears between the trees and, instead of an irate fairy, a beautiful autumn-colored Wolf is parked on the porch.

"Jack!" I squeal. And then I start running.

Chapter 6

Jack

Riley disappeared.

She vaporized right in front of my eyes in Phillip's garden two days ago. And she didn't come back.

I've been looking for her everywhere, following every little hint of her scent with my snout on the ground. But the entire forest smells of Red Riding Hood—it's impossible to tell if she was here today, last week, or two months ago. She didn't show up at either her or her grandma's place, but then Granny is supposed to be on vacation in Bedrock anyway. Both cottages are eerily empty, yet I keep running back and forth between them.

Every damn Short Message Stork I sent returned, telling me the message couldn't be delivered. According to them, she was either hiding underground or zapped to a part of the land that doesn't network with *E*-Apple yet—which, frankly, could be just about anywhere outside Grimmwich or the Wood of 1000 Dawns.

The third likely reason they gave me isn't an option I can accept… It would mean that Riley is lost. Forever. Gone from this world. Away from Fairyland.

It would mean that she stopped existing.

The thought kills me.

My latest roam of the forest was useless once again. I can smell her everywhere, but she never comes around the bend. The signpost that marks our first encounter in every repeat of our story is ahead. My paws are callused and hurting from running, so I stop and change back to my human self. Slowly, I walk to the post and lift my head to the four-way road signs, showing Plush Toy Forest, Grimmwich, Granny's House, and Glitter Hollow. Bile rises in my throat.

I recall when I first came here…when we didn't even have a story together. Damn, that was a long time ago…

I was hungry but too lazy to change into the Wolf and catch myself a deer for dinner. Someone told me that rabbits and pigs lived in the Plush Toy Forest. I sensed an easy meal there and almost headed off…if the sweet humming of a girl hadn't stopped me.

Curious about who was coming from the direction of Glitter Hollow, I leaned against the post and waited. And when that girl in a red cloak finally appeared, her lips curving into a shy smile as her steps faltered, her honey-colored eyes sparkling in the beams of sunlight pouring between the leaves, I knew I'd met my ever after—even if the real happy ending for me remained out of reach. But that was okay. Every story needed a villain. Just like they always need a fair maiden…

I shake myself out of my reverie. Since Riley disappeared from the ball, her merry tune has been constantly echoing in my ears. What I wouldn't give to hear her sing it again…

My eyes fall shut every so often. I haven't slept in forty-eight hours, and I wonder how much longer I'll be able to hold out. A short nap would probably be wise. Tearing my gaze away from the signpost, I tuck my hands into my pockets and shuffle off. But I don't want to go home. I can't. Not yet. Maybe never again, for a normal life without Riley is unthinkable.

As I follow the path to Glitter Hollow, my throat constricts more with every step I take. Swallowing hurts like hell. How can it be that every damn bush, every tree, and even the chirps of the birds in this part of the woods remind me of her?

Ahead of me is her little house. No smoke rises from the chimney today. All the windows are closed. The thought that she won't open the door when I knock lances my heart.

How could she do this to me? How could she just go and leave me alone?

My footsteps resound dolefully on the porch. Nothing has changed here since my last check this morning. Staring at the door for seconds on end, I slowly lift my hand. But it drops again without knocking. I try to swallow the lump in my throat that seems to have nested there for a lifetime. It doesn't go away. Helpless, I sink to my knees and finally change into the Wolf.

Because wolves don't cry.

My head lowers onto my front paws, and my eyes slide shut in exhaustion. For the first time in two days, I welcome sleep because it allows me to escape and not think about what my kiss might have done to Riley.

Oblivion sweeps me away, but it doesn't hold me down for long. Even in my dreams, her sweet humming haunts me, and it's so real that it pulls me back to consciousness. As I open my heavy eyelids, the tune is still there. Instinctively, my ears twitch in the direction of the sound. Could it be? Holding my breath, I lift my head and scan the path leading away from the house, but the humming stops. No one's there. I should have known.

About to drop my head again, a bolt of pure fire zaps through me as a familiar voice calls out my name. Frozen with hope—and panic at the same time that it's just my mind playing tricks on me again—I stare into the shadows of the trees.

And there she is. My happily ever after…running toward me.

My breath escaping in short pants, I jerk to my feet, once again taking my human form. One hand wound around the wooden post that supports the roof, I haul myself over the railing of the porch stairs to the ground and open my arms for her. Riley slams into me so hard that I grab her and stumble back a few steps at the impact. My arms tighten around her in a panicky hold.

"Why is everyone so happy to see me?" She laughs into my ear before I lower her to her feet again, but I still can't bring myself to ease the hug.

My eyes squeeze shut. It's so good to have her back. "I thought you were dead…" The words wrench out from my tight throat.

"Well, I'm not. And I don't plan to be anytime soon," she promises me in almost a whisper now, keeping her arms lightly around my neck. "You can let go."

I bury my face in her hair. "In a minute."

Riley's embrace gets a little stronger as her sigh brushes the skin of my neck. "I missed you, too, Jack."

A feeling like floating on clouds fills me as all the tension of the past couple of days eases out of my body. I can finally breathe again. And then a small hope grows in my chest. Just look at us—we are so much more now than we were a week ago. I don't know where she's been hiding for so long, but perhaps in the time she's been gone, she's come to understand how it is with us, too. Fooling her with the disguise of a prince and stealing a kiss was a stupid idea, but what if this is my second chance with her? Maybe we can start completely new again.

My fingers dig into her clothes. They feel strange somehow. Only then do I remember that she looked quite different when she walked out of the forest.

After several long seconds, I finally force myself to ease my tight hold on her waist and place my hands on her upper arms, moving her one step back for a better view. "Whose dress is this?"

Riley inhales deeply, and then her face splits with a grin. "You'll never believe what happened."

Oh, I think I just might.

"After you left Friday morning, I accidentally burned my dress, and then the Fairy Godmother came and gave me the gown from Cindy's story." Energetically, she grabs my arm and pulls me onto the porch as she babbles away. "That woman is bonkers and she"—her gaze falls to the shattered pieces of clay on either side of the door, and her enthusiasm wanes for a moment—"broke my plants."

This sounds like the intro to a seriously crazy night.

The querulous expression eases from her face. "Anyway, she turned my little bird fellow into a winged horse so I could get to the ball. And there, I met a real royal. Two, actually." Riley drags me inside and, with her bubbly voice filling the cottage, the place instantly feels warm and homey again. She pushes me onto the couch, obviously needing me to sit still and just listen. I don't complain. In fact, I watch with a smile as she hurries to the wardrobe in the back of the cabin where her bed is situated and takes out a few fresh items.

"Oh, the ball was so beautiful. You should have seen it, Jack," she rhapsodizes, coming back. Then her beam turns into a frown. "Where have you been, anyway? Your letter was quite cryptic."

Ugh. Unprepared, I bite my lip. She just returned from the dead. I don't want to lose her again because she hears the truth. It can wait. "Nowhere special. Just seeing a friend." To distract her from my lie, I wave a hand, urging her on. "So, the ball and the royal—there were two, you said?"

Fortunately, that's enough to push her into the next round of reporting. "Yes. One was a real scumbag. His name was Jaccomo Casanova, duke of some stupid land." Her face mars in disgust. "Have you heard of him?"

Slowly, I shake my head.

"Yeah, you haven't missed out on anything if you don't know him. But there was also Phillip's cousin, a prince." Her eyes glaze over as she sighs, pressing the pile of clothes to her chest and blinking at the ceiling. "He was a real dream lover."

Holy shit! I don't think I've ever been called that before. My lips twitch into a smile. "Thanks."

Riley returns from her castle in the clouds and stares at me for a second. "What?"

My smile falters. "*What...?*"

"You said 'thanks.' What for?"

"*Ugh...* I thought I heard you say I could get myself a glass of water." Quickly, I shake my head. "Never mind. Go on and tell me what happened at the castle."

"Oh...right." She frowns. Obviously, with my stupid *thanks* comment, she's completely lost the plot thread. "I need to take a shower real quick." She runs into the bathroom, calling over her shoulder, "Take whatever you want from the fridge." The door slams shut, but her voice drifts through the wood, muffled at times as she more than likely undresses. "The prince—his name is Jacob—danced with me, and then we took a walk through the gardens."

Water starts running in the shower, followed by her hysterical cry. "Whoa, cold!"

The image of her jumping backward all naked makes me chuckle. I rise and head to the sink, filling a glass from the tap while Riley continues her story. "He figured out that I was no princess, which was a bit of a shock. For me, not for him. He actually seemed quite comfortable with the thought of me not being a royal. We even talked about you, Jack."

I smile into the glass before I take a sip.

"And then we kissed. It was amazing. Aurora thinks he wants to marry me. Unfortunately, he had to go back to the Marble Mountains right after the ball, so I'll set off tomorrow to see him again."

The water in my mouth comes back out in a spray, dousing my shirt. *Fuck!* With the back of my hand, I rub my lips dry, shouting loud enough so she hears me through the door and over the sounds of the shower, "Why the hell would you do that?"

"To tell him '*yes, I do*,'" her dreamy drivel comes from the bathroom. "And to live in his castle as his happy wife forevermore."

She must be kidding. Grabbing a dishtowel from the counter, I hunker down and aggressively mop up the mess on the floor. "You talked to this guy for a few hours, and now you think you want to spend the rest of your life with him?"

"Yes."

"You know nothing about this dude."

"I know enough." Her snide voice drifts clearer through the door now since the running water has stopped.

"Really?" I snap, rising and dabbing at my wet t-shirt with the towel. "What's his tale?"

"I don't know."

"Is he the good guy or the bad guy of his story?"

A short pause. "That's not important."

"Does he have any diseases? Quirks? Can he even fight to protect you from danger?" I growl. "Is that unimportant, too?"

A cabinet door slams closed inside the bathroom. "You're just grumpy because you didn't believe me when I told you I'd find someone, and now I have."

She never thinks things through to the end, does she? "What if he's an imposter? An idiot dressing up as a prince to find a girl at the ball?"

The lock of the bathroom door clicks, and her voice is barrier-free again behind me as she grumbles, "You mean an idiot like me?"

"What?" I whirl around, and then my hands freeze in the middle of dabbing, my chin smacking down hard on my chest.

Riley stands before me in nothing but a fluffy white towel wrapped around her body, which she clasps together at the front. Water droplets slide down her naked legs, pooling at her ankles. Her wet hair cascades over her shoulders, some locks brushing the gentle curves of her breasts. *Holy fuck.*

"You said idiot." Her perfect eyebrows are drawn into a sable scowl. "I dressed up, too."

"No, that's not what I meant." Shit, my throat is as dry as a bone.

"I know what you meant." She takes a step closer. *Mmm, morning dew and wood strawberries...* Clutching the towel tighter to her chest with one hand, she points a reproachful finger at my face. "You thought the idea was stupid from the beginning."

Yes, I did, but for a completely different reason. "I think..." Damn, what was I going to say? With Riley wrapped only in a towel, my mind has been zapped into a fucking stupor.

"It doesn't matter what *you* think. I'll go and see Prince Jacob anyway. He loves me!"

This is ridiculous! Dropping the dishtowel, I grab her wrist and move her pointing finger out of my face. "How do you know that?"

With a challenging glare, she lifts her chin, her voice a provocative drawl, "Because he kissed me."

My teeth grit in frustration. As much as I love this girl, sometimes, she makes me want to bang my head against the wall. "You wouldn't know love if it rode over you with a carriage drawn by ten horses!" Without thinking, I slip my hand to the back of her neck, yank her closer, and press a rough kiss to her mouth.

Stunned, Riley gasps against my lips. No passion there today. *Of course.* And why should there be, I'm not a prince, am I? When she finally falls out of her stiffness, she smacks me on the chest and shrieks, "Jack! You're so...*argh*!" A deep frown slits her eyes. "Go home!"

My nostrils flare from breathing so hard, and my jaw works doggedly, but no words escape. Lips pressed together, I glare into her appalled eyes for several endless seconds. This girl understands exactly nothing! When her face remains hard as stone, I spin on my heels and stalk out the door. I slam it shut with so much force, the little cottage rattles from my frustration.

Chapter 7

Riley

Argh! Jack is such an impossible, pushy, stubborn…*Wolf.* How can he think that kissing me is the right way to end an argument? Did he really expect me to kiss him back? When I'm angry at him? And in love with someone else?!

Still wrapped in the bath towel, I slump onto the couch. As if I wouldn't recognize love. *Hah!* I've seen it often enough in my friends' stories. What happened between Jacob and me at the ball is *exactly* how a romance should go. Prince…girl…kiss. Duh!

It only shows that Jack has absolutely no clue.

Ignorant puppy dog. And here I even considered asking him to come with me to the Marble Mountains. I must have been out of my mind. He'll never understand. Rather than helping me find my happily ever after, he'll ruin it.

And what's with him running away in the middle of a fight? I was just shocked, I didn't really mean for him to leave when I said so. He should know that.

Folding my arms and lowering my chin, I glare holes into the door. He can go and play with the three little pigs for all I care. Maybe that'll make him happy. "Damn you, Jack! I don't need a flea-contaminated dog anyway!"

A sudden knock makes me jump where I sit on the couch.

Goodness, did he come back? Perhaps with an apology?

My heart clops in a flutter in my chest as I run to the door and yank it open. The next second, however, my hopeful face falls because, instead of the Wolf, there are forty or so storks in blue vests on my porch, and when they see me, they all start blaring a message.

*

Morning has just broken, and there's still the mist of dawn creeping around my house. It doesn't matter. In a few minutes, the sun will rise higher into the sky, waking the rest of Fairyland. I slip on my red cloak and pull up the hood. There is only one man I need to be awake right now anyway.

James Hook.

Even though Jack really got on my nerves yesterday, I still pin a note addressed to him to my door in case he comes back to apologize for being such a pighead. I don't want us to fight. If only he understood me a little better. A weary sigh escapes me because it's probably asking too much. We think too differently for that. I long for romance, while he doesn't want anything to change. No, we're not compatible at all…and that is sad.

But since my disappearance after the ball obviously distressed him, I don't want to leave without telling him where I'm going this time. To the Snow Plains—on foot, if there's no other choice. And with no idea when I'll be back, I also added a loving goodbye for him.

Yes, I did use the word *love*. He needs to know that, even if we're not a couple as prince and princess, he's still the person closest to me here in Fairyland. He always has been, and somehow, he will be forever.

But it's time to find out if there's something more out there.

I scurry out of the wood, head through Grimmwich, and go right to the Limping River Wharf. The imposing *Jolly Roger* sways gently on the sea. The white sails of the three-master are lowered, and no pirates scurry on deck this early in the morning. They're either asleep in their bunk beds in steerage, or they haven't returned from their nightly pub crawl yet. I cross my fingers that at least Captain Hook is on board.

A gangway leads from the concrete dock onto the ship. The wooden plank creaks and wobbles as I put a foot onto it. My gut churns. This is the first time I've been on any kind of boat. With a breath of panic stuck in my throat, I grip the ropes on either side of the plank harder. I'm not afraid of drowning if I fall into the water because I can swim. What scares the living shit out of me, though, is the eerie rocking of the vessel so close to the platform. If I slip and drop into the gap, I'll be mush.

Finally off the gangway, I scan the wide, empty deck. "Hello?" My voice is a timid tweep.

No answer. Up on the command bridge, the wheel is unmanned. The door beneath it leading to what I assume is the captain's cabin is closed. So are all the other doors on the far side of the ship, which must be the officers' quarters. They don't look exactly inviting, and a morning grouch is the last thing I need today. Nausea churns my stomach, but I'm not at all sure if it's from the fear of walking in the land of pirates or just from the movement of the vessel. It started at my first step onboard and increases with every second the ship bobs up and down in the gently rolling water.

Holy world under the sea! Just how can one live on a boat? I don't think I can stay on deck another minute. Whirling around to the gangplank to escape, a tall figure right in front of me stops me dead. "Whoa!" My hand flies to my heart. Where the hell did he come from?

Roguish blue eyes blink at me. "Can I help you, young lady?"

A dress shirt made of red linen hangs loosely over fitted leather pants. The buckles of his boots are polished to a gleam and blink in the first rays of the morning, and the stubble on his cheeks is just as black as his windblown hair. He plugs a massive silver hook into a fixture on his right wrist and, with a click, it locks. I guess I've found the captain.

"Yes. Well…" I push back my hood and hold out my hand. "Hello, Mr. Hook. My name is Riley Redcoat."

When he looks down at my hand and just smiles, I quickly pull it back and hold out the other one. Shaking hands with a silver hook probably wouldn't feel so pleasant. This time, he takes my palm and, even though his grip is gentle, it's tight enough that I can't remove my hand. "What brings you aboard my ship…little Red Riding Hood?"

Okay, so my cloak is probably a dead giveaway, just like his hook. That he doesn't let go of me makes me a little uncomfortable, and it adds to my nausea from the strange wobbling of the floor. I tug harder. "They say that you only sail to Neverland. Is that true?"

He gives me a stern nod. "Aye."

Why the heck doesn't he release my hand? "I urgently need to get to the North, but the only other ship sailed off yesterday, and the Storyteller knows when it'll be back."

"The *Dutchman* is usually gone for weeks," he

explains, head tilted.

"Yeah, that's what I feared." I take a tiny step sideways to balance out the rocking of the ship. Only then do I realize that I've been doing this little dance all along, and James is just holding me so I don't fall. Come to think of it, I probably wouldn't weather a cruise around the island very well anyway.

Struggling to find solid footing and keep my breakfast down, I tell him, "I plan on traveling to the Snow Plains through the country, but I have no idea which way to go. I was hoping you could help me. Do you have a map of Fairyland that you could lend me for the journey?" He was my best bet for this sort of thing because pirates always have maps of all possible islands on their ships, right?

He lifts an eyebrow. "You want to go to the Marble Mountains?"

"Mm-hmm."

"On foot?"

I nod.

His second brow moves up. "That's a three-day trek. Quite a long trip for a small girl like you."

I inhale deeply, squaring my shoulders. "It's about love."

A second ticks by then he chuckles. "Oh…love. That's a different matter, of course." Placing my hand in the crook of his arm, James Hook leads me to the quarters under the command bridge. "Let me see if I can find a map of Fairyland for you then."

The room is decked out in coffee-brown wood and appears very much like an office. A large desk looms in front of a row of square windows, allowing a glimpse of the blue waves stroking the horizon. Next to a cabinet stands an impressive globe with lots of islands in blue water. I spot names like Atlantis, Wonderland, and Lilliput on them. Neverland has a red note stuck on it. I can't read the scrawled words as James pulls me past the globe, but a skull is drawn on it, as well.

As soon as he lets go of me and walks to the cabinet, I grab the edge of the desk for support. My head jumps on a carousel hike…and so does my stomach.

The captain comes back with a map that he unrolls before me. He points a finger at the west shore of the light brown and green island that is Fairyland, surrounded by dark blue. "This is where we are now. If you want to go to the Snow Plains, you should take this route"—he runs his callused finger cross-country and up—"through Glimmergulf and then farther on across the meadows of Avalon. If you walk, it's another day through the Frosty Summits, and you better have enough provisions when you cross them. As far as I know, the last inn is at the border to the Marble Mountains."

It's all very interesting, but my mind is currently in a state of *I don't give a damn*. I lift a finger. "Excuse me." With a wonky smile, I gracefully stumble past him and then bolt outside. Where the hell are the toilets on this ship?

I realize I don't have time to go looking for them, so I fall against the railing, bend over, and puke into the sea.

A gentle hand touches my back, or maybe it's the backside of a hook, I don't know. "Your first time on a sea vessel?"

"Uh-huh."

James puts something into the inside pocket of my cloak. "You can keep this. We've got enough maps of the island on board."

Fighting my way to an upright position, I smile-grimace at him. "Thank you for this lovely conversation, Captain, but now I really must leave." Bile climbs up my throat once more, and I wheel around, letting another bout of vomit into the water. Ugh, don't eat blueberry muffins in the morning if you plan to be onboard a ship later.

When my stomach feels completely evacuated of my breakfast and any other meal I previously consumed, I zigzag across the deck, missing the gangplank to the wharf twice before I can get a fix on the exit. A hand on my back steadies me, and I push out a grateful sigh. James is a darling as he helps me on my way out.

Once back on solid ground, I drop flat on my stomach and cuddle the concrete. Oh boy, the cold cobblestones feel wonderful against my cheek. I'm sure they will make my head stop spinning in a minute.

"Are you all right?" The captain squats down next to me and angles his head low so we're almost at eye level. "Can I get you something? A glass of water, or a bucket perhaps?"

"No, I'm good. Just run on ahead and leave me behind. I'd like to die alone, thanks." I close my eyes as even the hard ground strangely rocks beneath me.

"What the fuck! Take your bloody hook off her!" The sharp voice, first from afar but coming closer really fast, kicks through me like a thunderbolt. Did somebody wave a bone, or why is the Wolf here?

My eyes stay sealed as boot heels sound next to me— the captain must have gotten to his feet. "Whoa, man, easy there. I didn't do nothin' with the lass."

"Sure! And that's why she's lying unconscious in the street, right?" Jack barks from somewhere above me. The next instant, I'm turned around. Strong hands shove beneath my body, and I'm lifted off the ground. "Are you okay, honeydrop?"

Ooh, he can be so gentle. My head rolls against his shoulder. "Maybe…not." I try to wrap my arms around his neck, but they are too weak to rise. Ah, what the heck, I'll just leave them where they are. Funny how fast his heart beats beneath my flat palm.

"Calm down, Wolf," James snarls from farther away now. "She came onboard and got sick. No permanent damage done, I'm sure."

"You better pray it is so, Hook." Lethal…he sounds so lethal. I want gentle Jack back. And then I want to sleep. Good Grimm, I'm so giddy.

"He told the truth," I moan. "It's not the captain's

fault. The sea is just no place for me."

With a brief shift, he adjusts me in his arms. "Don't worry, I'll get you out of here."

Eyes still squeezed shut, I hope someone switches off the merry-go-round in my head—and soon. Besides, being transported this way doesn't make things a whole lot better. "Jack..." I claw at his shirt. "You need to stop the wobbling, or I'll puke on your shoulder."

Silently, he carries me a few more steps, then he holds me tighter as we lower down somewhere. For the briefest moment, I open my eyes to cast a glance around. Obviously, we're sitting on the ground. Somewhere under a lonesome tree on a hill with the shore far below us. Well, he is on the grass—I'm actually nestled on his lap, cuddled against his chest. Okay, we're cool now. I can survive in this position.

Minutes pass, and all is silent and peaceful. The fragrance of grass and apple trees soothes my nausea. Along with something else—a scent I know so well, yet something I was never really aware of. I inhale deeply. "Why do you smell like snowdrops, Jack?"

The breath of his quiet laugh brushes my cheek. "Do I?"

"I don't know. But your scent reminds me of them."

He straightens a little and nestles his chin on top of my head. "Maybe because I lie in the moss a lot when I'm the Wolf."

Makes sense. Insecurity makes my face scrunch, and I

open my eyes, my gaze following the flightpath of a purple butterfly. "Can you smell me, too?"

"Mm-hmm."

"What do I smell of?"

"Morning dew and wood strawberries." I like his laid-back voice when he says it. It sounds like he quite enjoys the scent.

"Granny always makes me shampoo and body wash from them."

Jack wraps his arms a little tighter around me. "You might have to leave a bottle here for me when you ride off for your new ever after."

Shifting my head so I can look up at his face, I grin. "And I'll have to keep a bunch of beagle-whelps in my new castle to remind me of you."

His eyes glint with mischief as he smirks for a quiet moment, and then a pinch on my side makes me squeal. Laughing, I bury my face against his shoulder. Jack doesn't move. He just keeps me cuddled against him. I never believed this would actually feel so comfortable.

"Riley?" he says after another quiet moment of just resting his chin on my head again.

"Hmm?"

"Why were you on Hook's ship this morning?"

"Because I needed to borrow something from him." Absently, my hand slips into the inside pocket of my cloak to feel for the map there. "I don't know the way to the Snow Plains."

His chest lifts with two long breaths. "So you still want to follow this prince to the Marble Mountains?"

That's my plan, yes. But my heart squeezes a little at his disappointed undertone. "Jack...I really like you, I do. You've become such an amazing friend these past few days, which I'm incredibly thankful for. But with Jacob, it's different. I have never been in love before." A sigh leaves me. "Maybe you were right yesterday—maybe I don't know if the feelings I have for him are real love. But I need to figure it out. For myself. Can you understand that?"

After a very long time, I feel his slow nod on my head. "And if you don't find what you're looking for there?"

All through last night, that thought played around and around in my mind. What if I was mistaken and Jacob didn't fall for me? Jack's harsh words in my house yesterday started an unpleasant string of doubts. Or maybe it was the kiss he staggered me with...

I never believed that we had room for any kind of romantic feelings in our story. We've known each other way too long for that. If there were deeper affections, they'd have shown themselves somewhere along the way, wouldn't they?

But sitting here with him now...like this...just holding onto each other... It's amazingly nice. And suddenly, the entire prince hunt feels strangely exhausting. I close my eyes. "If there isn't true love waiting for me in the Snow Plains, I'll come back, and we'll be what we've always been. Red Riding Hood and the Wolf. I'll stop looking for a different ever after then."

Jack slips his hand into my hair and presses me tenderly against him. "You promise?" he whispers.

I crawl deeper into his embrace. "I do."

Chapter 8

Jack

Later that day, in front of Aurora's palace, I lift Riley into the saddle. When I asked Phil about a ride for the honeydrop, so she doesn't have to walk the entire way, he offered up the white mare because Riley is an inexperienced rider, and Lucinda is his safest horse.

I still have no idea how she swayed me into coming along on this madcap journey. Why I didn't just tell her the truth about Jacob this morning under the apple tree on the hill…

Phillip has a theory. He thinks when it comes down to

our girls, all men—Wolf or prince—are just the same: stupid cowards. Even after all these years, Rory obviously still believes that the beautiful ice sculpture of the unicorn that the Ice Queen gave them for their wedding fell in a storm. The seventeen-feet-high figure towered in front of their castle for centuries…until Phillip rode his coach home drunk one morning and mowed it down.

He could be right about the wimp thing. There were enough chances to tell Riley the truth about the ball and Jacob, but in the end, I simply turned tail. It's partly due to the letter that was stuck on her door when we arrived back at her house to pack the supplies this morning. When I read my name on it, I snatched it before she could. And after skimming through it, my mind was set.

She said she'll come back to be just *us* again if Jacob isn't what she expects. And he won't be because, well…he doesn't exist.

All I have to do now is take her to the Marble Mountains and back again. She'll never find out that Jacob is, in fact, a Wolf in prince's clothing. She won't hate me. And even if she can't love me the way I love her, she'll still be mine. I can settle for that.

Instead of her usual bow and quiver, a backpack with enough food and water for the next two days hangs on Riley's shoulders. Her red cloak fans out beneath it and covers the white mare's back. I zip up my leather jacket, then smack Lucinda on the behind and, when she starts off in a gentle gallop, I change into the Wolf and run alongside them.

Oh, man, I pray I don't end up in Hades' realm for doing this.

Soon, we're out of the Wood of 1000 Dawns and traveling on through Glimmergulf. It's a small, busy valley, and elves and leprechauns wave at us from all possible ends. Beyond it stretch the meadows of Avalon. As far as the eye can see, there's only grassland and knobby, old trees, and a mystical spark clings to the air that makes my hackles stand on end.

Riley slows the horse as the land descends into darkness. We've been on the road for hours. An alluring song drifts from Loch Wrinkle, the magical waters that have spawned countless mermaids and nymphs for all kinds of fairy tales. Over in the shadows of thirteen weeping willows, tall figures in long robes and hoods wander with candles through an ominous white fog around the lake.

"The Fays," she whispers in awe.

Straightening into my human self, I grip the reins and lead the mare in a wide berth around the lake. A disappointed expression crosses Riley's face, but whatever the fairies and druids are doing over there, we better not waltz into their party.

When the songs fade far behind us, and the trees tighten to a forest in front, I stop the horse and ask, "Can I see the map again?"

Riley pulls it from her coat and hands it to me. Unfolding it in the blue moonlight, I hunt down Avalon and Loch Wrinkle to figure out where we need to go next. It's good to see that we've already completed more than half the journey to the Marble Mountains. Without the horse, we'd probably just have come out of Glimmergulf by now.

"It's only a half-mile through the forest," I tell Riley, twisting around to catch the best light on the map and avoid my own shadow. "Behind lies the Rhymeshire, and in about an hour, we should reach Minvendeen's Edge. It's the last town before the Marble Mountains. We'll head there and spend the night."

"Do you hear that?" Riley pats the mare's neck. "We're almost there. Soon, you can eat and rest."

Mist pools around Lucinda's nostrils as she snuffles—and I swear, around Riley's nose, too. She must be just as tired as the horse.

I hand Hook's map back to her and change into the Wolf again. It's not only to reach the small town at the other side of the Rhymeshire faster, but I've never been to this part of Fairyland before. No one knows what kind of creatures dwell here. I like to be prepared for trouble, especially having Riley with me.

As we emerge from the thicket of the woods minutes later, the faint lights of Minvendeen's Edge beckon us in the distance. We follow a winding road until the dirt under our feet gives way to cobblestones. Lucinda's hooves clack on the narrow street, the sound echoing in the night. Back in human form, I lift Riley down from the horse and take the backpack off her shoulders. With a relieved moan, she rolls her neck and straightens her spine.

Shouldering the backpack myself now, I give her an encouraging smile. "We're almost there. At the end of Ruby Street, there should be an inn where we can stay."

She nods and hides her face deep inside the red hood as we start walking.

Tall houses with pointed roofs close us in, and warm light falls onto the road from countless windows, brightening our path. Several evening strollers dressed in frocks and elegant dark gowns greet us. The men lift their top hats or just tap them with the handholds of their canes as they pass us. Even the women wear hats in this place, most adorned with flowers, feathers, or silk loops.

In front of a snug, two-story tavern with filigree wrought-iron-framed windows and a wide stable attached to the side, we finally halt. The entrance is quite busy with people walking in and out of the place. Every time the door opens, a quick wave of music and merry chatter drifts to us. Above the front door, a wooden sign on brass fittings creaks as it swings in the Neverwind of the Rhymeshire. Moonlight glints off the name written in quirky golden letters.

The Copper Gauntlet.

We tie Lucinda to a post between a black warhorse with iron armor and a brindle pony, then unbuckle the saddle and place it on a nearby corbel. She happily drinks from a trough and feasts on a mound of hay. She's in good company for the night. While Riley pats her neck and says goodnight, I cast a look around. If these warm stables are anything to go by, the pub should be a cozy place.

"Come on. You must be hungry, too." I hold out my arm to Riley, which she gladly takes, and we head to the front of the tavern where I open the door for her. Her mouth drops open as she enters, and she freezes, looking around in wide-eyed fascination. She's probably never set foot in such an establishment before.

To me, the pub doesn't look a whole lot different than the *Shady Wonders* in Grimmwich. Maybe a little more old-fashioned. Tables of dark wood in various sizes with benches on either side crowd the place. Beneath the stairs leading up to the guest rooms is the bar, and there's even a lonely pool table in the back near the minstrel quartet. The acrid bite of pipe-smoke is just as familiar as the smell of ale and wine.

When her standing and gaping starts to draw the attention of a group of rowdies in dark robes and turbans, I grab her arm and pull her to a private corner with a table for two. Someone dropped the name Ali Baba as we came in, and I want to avoid having forty thieves snooping around my girl.

The innkeeper comes along, wiping his hands on the dirty white apron around his protruding belly, and lights the candle on our table to brighten the small space. Waving his hand, he extinguishes the match and tosses it carelessly to the ground. "What can I get you?"

I drop my leather jacket on the backpack and slide the bundle between my feet under the chair before reaching for the menu. There aren't a lot of drinks on it suited for Riley. I'd prefer a raspberry sherbet for her instead of whisky, but from what I see here, she can have water or a drunken stupor by the end of the night. At least the variety of foods offered is immense.

Riley orders pheasant and potatoes, while I go for a bloody boar steak. For drinks, we share a jug of water.

A little later, the innkeeper comes back with our meals, and not a minute too early. Judging by the vast rumble of Riley's stomach, she might have started chewing on the table if he hadn't. On that account, it surprises me when she begins to courtly pick at the roasted bird with a fork and a knife instead of just digging in. Getting meat off the drumstick obviously causes her trouble as they are just mini-bites she feeds herself with.

I watch for a moment and then laugh. "Goodness, Riley, you're such a barbarian. How can you torture your food like this?" From what I see, there are only three other women in the tavern, and neither of them pays heed to etiquette with their meals. I don't know where she thinks we landed, but if she sits any straighter, the innkeeper's St. Bernard might mistake her for a bone.

"Why? How would *you* eat that?" she snaps, clearly frustrated with her progress on settling her hunger.

I reach over and tear the entire leg out of the pheasant. Provocatively bracing my elbow on the table, I hold the drumstick right in front of her face.

Her cheeks reddening to match her cloak, she casts a bashful look around. People stare back at us, but certainly not because we're the wild ones. "If you don't want to stand out, take the drumstick and eat like a Wolf," I tease her and wink.

She runs her tongue across her lip, then swallows.

One eyebrow lifted, I wave the drumstick like an invitation until she finally takes it out of my hand. With her gaze lowered, she sinks her teeth into the roasted meat, her stomach approving with yet another rumble, loud enough to shake the inn.

Wiping my hands clean on the cloth napkin, I chuckle and then continue devouring my steak. Riley isn't the only one starving tonight.

Done and full half an hour later, we both shove our empty plates away. "That was…*nice*," she says, her eyes sparkling with surprise. "Wolf-style is definitely the better way to eat pheasant."

I lean forward, take her napkin, and wipe a tiny smudge of gravy from her cheek. "You'd make a fine Wolf, Red Riding Hood." Before drawing my hand back again, I nudge her chin with my knuckle and smile.

Quickly, she licks her fingers and wipes the spot I just cleaned three more times. "Gone?"

"Gone." Chuckling, I lean back.

"Don't laugh…" She throws a wary glance around us. "I can't look like a filthy pig. We're in company here."

That cracks me up completely. "Oh, and what a *fine* company it is." I roll my eyes. But even with gravy on her face, she could never look like anything but the red angel from the forest to me. My red angel with the honey eyes.

Thinking of honey... "Do you want anything for dessert?"

Lips compressing, she shakes her head and rubs her tummy. "I don't think there's room left for more."

I lift my hand and shout for the innkeeper anyway. It's time to make arrangements for the night. While he comes over, I fetch a few silvers from my jeans' pocket and place them on the table. He swipes the coins into his hand then drops them into his apron. "I hope everything was to your satisfaction?"

"Absolutely." I brace myself on my folded arms while he stacks the plates. "We would like a room for the night—two rooms."

The gray-haired man looks up. "Sorry, we're almost booked up. I can offer you one room. The Winter Suite. It has two beds, if that's all right with you."

I wouldn't mind, but who knows what Riley thinks about it. Arching my brows at her in question, I wait. After a second, she nods and turns to the innkeeper, who's still holding our plates. "We'll take it."

"Very well. I'll bring you the key in a minute." With a firm nod, he walks off and disappears into the kitchen. Moments later, on his way back to us, he grabs a brass key from the board behind the bar and drops it in my hand.

I start playing with the small wooden plate hanging from it, etched with the golden number 7. "Can you tell us how we get to the Snow Plains from here?"

He snorts as he tilts his head. "Did you come on foot?"

"No, a horse."

"Well, you can only travel on foot from here on." He runs a hand through his shaggy hair. "The way is steep and stony. Not fit for a horse's legs."

Riley frowns. "How long until we reach the Snow Plains then?"

Staring into the candle flame, he thoughtfully rubs his whiskered chin. "Three-quarters of a day for the ascent to the Frosty Summits, I'd say. There is a reindeer shelter up there with enough straw and hay to make a fine camp. You best stop there for the night because it'll be the last place to warm yourself before another half-day's worth of hiking through the snow." He scrutinizes Riley and then gives me a serious look. "Maybe a bit longer for the lass."

I nod.

"For a silver a day, you can leave your horse here until you come back. I'll take good care of the animal."

"Thanks. We'd appreciate it." And Phillip surely would, too.

"May I ask what you seek in the Snow Plains? Visitors usually come by ship from the north side."

"Yeah, ships are a minor problem." I grimace at the memory of Riley's green face at the Limping River Wharf this morning. "Just visiting the place. They're said to be beautiful."

"Pretty, they certainly are, but deadly, too. Do you have an invitation to the king's castle? For there's not much else up there in the ice lands to find shelter from the crystal storms. Other than some cold grottos, that is."

I swallow. "There's really a royal family housed there?" The words are out before I think twice.

Riley throws me a *duh* glare. "Told you so." Then she beams at the innkeeper with her ever-charming smile. "I met Prince Jacob at a ball last weekend. He'll surely be happy to see me again."

"Prince Jacob?" His bushy brows quirk. "The king is known as Alexander the Great in this region."

Riley's smile fades a little. "Maybe Jacob is his son?"

"He definitely has no sons, for he has no wife. The king barely comes out of his empire, and no lass has voluntarily braved the cold to live with him yet." He rasps a throaty laugh. "Are you sure you're searching in the right spot for your prince?"

"Yes…" Looking as if she needs some comfort, she wraps her cloak tighter around herself. "He said he came from the Snow Plains. But it was a masked ball." Her hopeful gaze switches to mine. "Do you think he used a fake name for cover?"

I focus on the knotholes in the table because I can't look into her eyes anymore. "Possibly."

"If he did so to win your heart and bait you up here,

young lass," the innkeeper says with quite some enthusiasm, "you should give the cold a chance. No matter what the stories say about him, King Alexander is one of the finest men fairy kind has ever spawned. He deserves a good woman at his side."

After he leaves us alone with a merry chuckle on his lips, Riley reaches across the table and grabs my hand, excitement ringing in her voice. "Did you hear that? Alexander must be Jacob! He obviously didn't want to be recognized at the ball. Oh, he's such a sweet thing. And I don't mind some snow outside the house."

My blood ices in my veins. Fuck, what have I done?

She might not find Jacob in the Marble Mountains, but she might find someone who'd gladly welcome her into his kingdom. And with her determination to marry a royal and write her new happily ever after, she won't care who the castle owner is in the end. I take a big gulp of water, hiding my panic behind the glass. If only I could drown myself in it right now.

"Jack, what's that thing over there?"

Grateful for the distraction, I trace the path of Riley's outstretched arm. "It's a pool table. You never played?"

"No. What do you play on it? Memory?"

I look back at her and, despite the horror I'm doubtlessly going to face over the next couple of days, I laugh. "No, not memory. It's a game with balls. You wanna try it?"

She nods avidly, so I grab the backpack from the floor

and rise. As we walk past Ali Baba's table, an uncomfortable number of eyes fasten on Riley. I lay an arm possessively around her shoulders. Fixing all forty thieves and *him* with a lethal glare, a deadly growl pushes from my throat.

If their life is dear to them, they better not even think about touching my girl.

"Hey, there are no balls." Riley's voice tears my attention away from the Arabian gang. "Did someone steal them?"

"No, they come from this opening. Watch." I pull the lever to release the fifteen balls plus the white one. As they rumble down, I pull them from the removal window and place them on the crimson felt.

"Cool. And now what? Do we try to roll them into one of the holes in the table?" She snatches the yellow ball and gives it a sharp push diagonally across the table where it drops into a hole. Then she jumps with joy. "Look at that! I scored!"

While she reaches for the next one in her sweet excitement, I grab her hand, holding it tenderly as I fix her eyes with mine. "That is not how you play pool, honeydrop."

"No?"

Shaking my head, I let her go, walk around the table, and set up the balls in a triangle, fetching the yellow one from the removal window again. The cues are on a stand nearby. "Stay here. Don't touch anything," I warn her then get a cue for myself and a shorter one for her. "So the goal is to run either the fully colored balls or the striped ones into the pockets, using only the white ball and this stick to shoot it."

"And that works?" Her face crumples with skepticism. "Sounds quite complicated to me."

I smooth the tip of my cue with the blue chalk. "It does, with a little practice. Come on, I'll show you." After putting the chalk cube aside, I line up the white ball in front of the triangle formation and lean down with the cue in position. A hard thrust, and the balls scatter, hitting the other end of the table, one rolling neatly into the back left pocket—as always.

"Oh no!" Riley squeals, her face torn with disappointment as she clutches her heart. "The red ball is the prettiest one. Why did you sink it first?"

She never ceases to raise my smirk. The cue's grip on the floor, I grab it with both hands, bracing my weight on it as I casually lean in to her ear. *Because…it is the prettiest one.*"

As I straighten again, Riley's shy gaze finds mine and holds me captive. Her breathing steady and deep, she blinks so slowly that it makes me feel as if time has stopped around us. And then the softest of smiles appears on her lips.

To stop myself from just cupping her face and kissing her right then, I clear my throat. "Would you like to try it now?"

She nods. "Can I do the black one?"

"Uh-uh." Lips compressed, I shake my head. "If you do, you lose."

"Why?"

"The number eight is always the last ball to sink."

"So you can sink red, but I can't sink black?" Her petite brows tip down into a disapproving V. "What kind of stupid rule is that?" Bending over the table, she aligns herself in almost the same position I was in before—and, of course, she's going after the eight ball. I throw my head back and laugh.

Riley struggles to keep the tip of the cue still and not miss the white ball completely.

"Do it like this." Leaning in from the side, I spread her left hand on the felt and show her how to run the upper end of the cue through her fingers. "The index finger on top to secure it and then give it a smooth stroke."

When she's got that part figured out, the next problem is her cloak. It keeps sliding forward, no matter how often she tosses it back over her shoulders. A muscle works in her jaw. Red Riding Hood is losing her temper. In the end, even the hood falls over her head.

Biting back my chuckle now, I gently take the cue out of her hand and put it aside. Apparently not happy with that, she straightens, but I ignore her confusion and slide in front of her. Leaning back against the table, I pull her a little closer, my legs slightly parted so she can stand between them. "This won't work."

Her gaze is boring into me. It's tangible, yet I keep my focus on the button that holds her cloak closed at the collar. She doesn't protest when I carefully slip it free, holding the two sides of the satin. Slowly, I brush the garment over her shoulders, and only then do I look into her eyes again.

Still clasping the fabric, my fingers slide down her arms until our hands meet. I run my knuckles over her warm skin and eventually intertwine our fingers, the cloak's ends between our palms.

An unspoken question lingers behind Riley's eyes. Grimm only knows what rode me to do this. When she doesn't back away, my gaze falls to her lips and, suddenly, all I can think of is how sweet they tasted during our very first kiss. My head lowers.

Don't do it! Don't do it! Don't do it!

Yesterday, in her hut when I tried to give her a glimpse into my feelings for her, she pushed me away and told me to go home. I can't risk making the same mistake again today, for the way home is far and long.

But damn, her lips beg to be devoured. I drag her even closer…and she doesn't resist.

"Excuse me," a deep voice breaks into our moment. "Do you still intend to play this game?"

Brutally ripped out of a bubble where Riley and I really could be more than just friends, my head snaps around to face a tall sorcerer with a pointed hat, a shaggy white beard, and a long gray robe. He holds a stick as tall as himself in one hand, and a woman in a deep blue velvet dress in the other.

I need a moment to shake myself out of my stupor. "No. We're done." A cold shower is safer than staying here with Riley anyway.

I release her hands, grab the backpack from the floor, and sling it over one shoulder before ushering her away from the table.

"Come on, Morgana," the man simpers behind us. "It's time for revenge."

Leaving the bar parlor, I drag Riley up the stairs with me, giving her no time to object or even ask questions. Room number seven is on the second landing. The key slides in easily.

"I wonder why they call it the Winter Suite," she murmurs beside me.

As the door swings open, a frosty wind wafts in our faces.

Hesitating a moment, I turn a raised eyebrow at her. "I guess that's your answer."

"Ooh, it's cold." Riley wraps her cloak around herself as she enters first. The next instant, she swirls around and jumps backward onto one of the two beds with its white sheets, bouncing up and down, her face splitting into a grin. "But I like it."

"It'll do." Why they call the teensy-weensy room a suite totally escapes me, though. There's nothing in this loft, other than those wooden-frame beds with a chest and an open window between them. The roof slopes down on the other side of the room, making sure we can only stand upright in this section.

I drop the backpack onto the other bed and head for the second door in the room. It leads into a very small bathroom with a toilet and a glass shower cubicle. "Mind if I take a shower first?" I ask her, kicking off my shoes. I still need that cold shower to stop the crazy feelings from five minutes ago.

She waves her hand. "Go ahead."

I close the door and pull off my black t-shirt, tossing it onto the mini sink next to the toilet.

"Oh my Goodness, Jack!"

The panicked shriek from outside makes me jump right against the door of the shower. Shit! Flooded with pain and terror, I yank the door open and rush outside. "Riley?!"

But no Rhymeshire troll or any such thing has come to kidnap her from the room. She stands by the window, both hands lifted as she looks at the ceiling seemingly in deep wonder. "It started when I closed the win—" Her voice breaks off the moment she lowers her gaze to me. There's something white clinging to her lashes as she blinks. Only then do I realize it's snowing. In. The. Room!

"What the hell?" My brows drawn down, I stride to the square port in the wall and open it again. Immediately, the snowing stops. Another test run proves that it'll restart any time someone shuts the damn window. "So you have a choice between cold and colder in this room," I deadpan.

Riley nods. Slowly. Her mouth is slightly ajar, her gaze fixed on my chest.

"Is everything okay?" She seems to be caught in a daze. Is my fly open? I check and find that my jeans are closed, but my abs twitch from the cold, and my nipples are hard like diamonds. As I look up again, Riley is still gaping. A small smirk tugs at the corner of my mouth. "What?" Could it be that she's never seen a half-naked guy before?

She swallows, and her cheeks turn red.

That sparks my chuckle. Chin dipped low, I prowl toward her and nudge her snub nose. "Cute reaction." Then I make sure to gently brush against her as I slip past her and head back into the bathroom.

Winter Suite, my ass.

Chapter 9

Riley

Jack confuses me. His nearness confuses me. Heck, even his *naked body* confuses me.

While he opens and closes the window to figure out what's defective with the air conditioner in the room, my gaze is totally nailed to his firm, chiseled chest. The muscles beneath his flawless skin twitch as he moves. Beautiful. My fingers itch to run along the edges and valleys between each individual muscle. Don't judge me, I live in the woods. Naked men don't just rove around there.

When he comes away from the wall and talks to me,

his words barely register. The only thing my mind can do is connect his deep, familiar voice to this gorgeous body. And then he smirks and flicks my nose. "Cute reaction."

To what? The snow? Was I dancing? I haven't seen snow before, but right now, I can't tell which of the two is more intriguing—the fluffy white flakes or Jack's bare chest. Can I just rub some snow on his body, please?

Admittedly, this room isn't the biggest, but we're alone in here, darn it, and yet he manages to crowd me on his way back to the bathroom. The strangest thing is that I find I like it. It's like some complex, unnamed game we've been playing since he tried to teach me pool. One where he's testing how quickly he can dumbfound me. Apparently, he knows all the right tricks, too.

Earlier, when he pulled me between his legs down in the pub and laced our fingers, I got caught up in the memory of a very pleasant feeling. The warm image of me sitting cradled on his lap under the tree this morning danced before me. For a brief moment, I wanted to cuddle up to him again.

Only, in the next breath, I realized that I was standing with someone else in almost that same position not long ago. With Prince Jacob in the castle garden. He gave me a whole different feeling then…and yet, they were so similar.

Shaking my head to abandon the confusion, I turn around. The door to the bathroom is closed, and running water inside proves that Jack is already in the shower. I better not think about what the rest of him looks like naked, or the woozy feeling in my head will never go away again.

It's pretty cold in the room, even though the snowing stopped when Jack left the window ajar. By just sitting around on the bed, doing nothing, I'll freeze my butt off. Maybe a quick visit to the stables to visit Lucinda would be better. That place certainly seemed cozier than this room.

A bowl with fresh fruit sits on the chest between our beds. I pocket two green apples and run down the stairs, exiting the inn to head for the horse shelter. While the tavern still bustles with guests and bursts of merry laughter escape, the big main gate of the stables has been closed. A sign points to the alley beside it where, apparently, there's another door for the riders.

It's murky outside and gets even darker as I round the corner. A chilly breeze wafts through my hair and stirs my cloak. Everybody knows the legends of the Neverwind—it carries the souls of new stories born here in the land of rhymes, all across our world. Still, I didn't imagine the Rhymeshire to be such a cold place at night. With my cloak drawn tightly around me, I search for the door.

"May we help you, little one?"

A shudder zips through me at the devious voice, the tone absolutely not matching the innocent question. My gaze zeroes in on the end of the alley, and I freeze. Two men, both wearing headscarves and dark tunics with black rag pants and desert boots, emerge from the shadows. The sneers on their faces turn my blood cold—along with the saber one of them holds.

I swallow. "No thanks. I was just thinking about going back to the tavern." My voice is the copy of a creaking door. "Good evening."

The second one with a thin line of black beard along his angular jaw draws a glinting blade from the sheath at his hip and tilts his head. "I don't think we want you to leave just yet."

Instinctively, I reach to my back to draw my bow and an arrow but…dang, all I brought with me on this journey is the stupid backpack. And not even that is here right now so I could throw it at the thugs and run. There's no knife in my boot either because it's still stuck on the door of my cottage where I pinned the letter for Jack earlier this morning.

Good job, Red Riding Hood.

In a panic, I mentally race through my options, and that leaves me with the apples in my cloak pocket. Crud! I reach for them and haul my arm back, trying to use my narrowed eyes as additional weapons. But heck, how do you look mean and deadly? My mouth compresses into a tight line, and I draw my brows down until my face feels crampy.

The one with the beard lowers his blade and laughs, holding his tummy. "Seriously?"

Yes.

The other one just snickers as he draws closer. "Keeping nice treasures in that cloak of yours. We might have to go on a raid through your clothes and see what else you're hiding."

"Don't come near me!" I screech, fear paralyzing me.

"Or else? Are you going to hurt us, poppet? All by yourself?" he drawls as they both take slow steps forward, their faces hardening into perilous miens. "Where's your watchdog now, hm? The one with the fine snarl?"

"Right here." The air around us freezes at the deadliness of the voice coming from behind me.

I can only move so much to look over my shoulder, my bones shaking like leaves. "Jack," I whisper.

He slowly walks forward from the shadows, fixing me with commanding eyes. "Get back inside." As if pushed by the insistency of his voice alone, I withdraw two steps, but then I freeze again, watching as he changes into the mighty autumn-colored Wolf right in front of me.

Never breaking his deadly stride, he aims for the two sinister figures, baring his teeth. Their faces turn white like chalk, but they quickly recover and hold their weapons in defense before them. "Bad mistake, Wolf," one of them spits.

They don't get to say more because Jack leaps, and I scream in terror, backing into the wall. He bowls them down, rolling across the alley with both men. Barks and snarls erupt along with cussing and shouting. The men slash at the Wolf with their sabers, while Jack only has his teeth and claws to fight.

Terrified, I press the two apples into my chest. All I

can think of is how badly I want to go back to the Wood of 1000 Dawns right now because people don't try to kill each other there.

The Wolf is on top of one Arabian thug as the other rushes at him from behind. The moonlight hits his blade in a mortal gleam as he swings.

"Jack, watch out!" I cry and, in a panic, fling an apple at the sneaky attacker, hitting him right on the head. It doesn't knock him out, but his gape of surprise is enough for Jack to turn around and clamp his fangs around the man's calf.

The battle turns deadlier than ever, the three of them merging into one never-ending bundle of arms, legs, teeth, and sabers. They plow across the alley where the shadows swallow them up. It's killing me that I can't see what's going on any longer, I can only hear their mean voices and the rustles on the ground as they roll even farther away. Moments later, a sharp howl breaks through the night, and the sound stops my heart. Then there's only silence…

As if under a spell, my breath caught in my lungs, I stand rigid, my gaze fixed on the darkness at the end of the alley. Nothing moves in the shadows. "Jack?" There's barely any sound coming from my throat. My fingers dig into the remaining apple so hard that sticky juice trickles down my hand. Cautiously, I take a few steps down the street, every inch of me rebelling at the thought of finding my friend dead after the battle. While he was protecting me. If there's really something like a star to wish upon, then please let Jack be all right! Tears mist my sight. "Please, say something."

Movement in the darkness makes me stiffen again. A figure looms there just at the edges. I suck in a sharp breath as an icy coldness creeps into my bones. The apple still fisted tightly in my hand, I'm prepared to fire it at whoever is lurking in the shadows. "Stay where you are. I'm armed."

The next instant, a shockwave of relief loosens all my invisible ties as a Wolf limps toward me. I dash forward, throwing my arms around his neck as I fall to my knees. The apple bounces away on the cobblestones.

I bury my hands and face in his fur, rubbing and cuddling him while hard sobs break free from my throat. "Goodness, Jack, I thought I lost you!"

And suddenly, a very recent line that I heard from him rings eerily in my ears. *I thought you were dead.* Jack had me fearing for his life for only minutes, but when I was unconscious at Dorothy's house, he didn't know what had happened to me for two full days. Only now I begin to understand what he must have gone through in that time. I cuddle him tighter and run my hands over his head a few times, flattening his ears with the motion.

Jack shifts back to a man in my embrace, yet I can't bring myself to let him go. "Why are you still here?" he rasps, his forehead resting on my shoulder, his arms wrapped firmly around me. "I told you to get back inside."

"And I didn't listen," I snivel. "What do you want to do about it? Eat me?"

A soft breath pushes through his nose as he shoves his hand into my hair. "No…" Then he presses a tender kiss to my temple, and I close my eyes.

When something wet lands on my forearm, soaking into my blouse, my gaze falls down. A big red spot spreads out on the white fabric. I pull away from Jack and scan his arm under the sleeve of his black t-shirt. A deep cut runs across his biceps. "By all good fairy tales! What did they do to you?"

"It's nothing, just a scratch."

"Yeah, and the Jabberwocky is a cuddly lizard." I push his hand away as he tries to shield the wound from my eyes and dab at it with the corner of my cloak. Sheesh, that looks nasty.

Sitting in the street, Jack lets me work on his injury, his eyes fixed on my face rather than his arm. I only lock gazes with him briefly, then I tear a strip from my cape and bandage his wound with it. "Do you think that'll work?"

He cups my chin and makes me look at him once more. "Don't worry. I heal fast."

After a long moment, a slow, deep breath eases my chest and gives my heart room to unclench. My fingers wrap around his wrist, squeezing gently. "I'll always worry about you."

Jack smiles. He stands up, slips his wrist from my grip, and then takes my hand, pulling me to my feet. He doesn't let go as we walk back to the tavern.

Inside, my gaze skates across the bustling place. The

group of men with headscarves and tunics is still having a merry time, drinking and laughing at their table in the back. Two seats near them are empty now, though.

A sudden ball of unease settles in my stomach. In the middle of ascending the creaky stairs leading to the landing of our room, I yank Jack to a halt.

He stops one step above me, scrutinizing me with a lifted eyebrow.

I grimace. "You didn't eat the two thugs in the alley, did you?"

For a long, worrisome moment, he just stares at me, then he ruffles my hair and drags me on.

What the heck? "Yes, or no?" I demand, stalking up behind him because he can't just gobble up freaking characters.

Gently, he pushes me into our luxurious, snowy Winter Suite and laughs. "Now, wouldn't you love to know, Red Riding Hood?"

Great. No answer on that front. I turn around to him as he closes the door. "How did you know where to find me anyway?"

His amusement vanishes. "The room was empty when I came out of the shower, fruit was gone from the bowl"— he nods at the chest under the ajar window—"and you weren't down in the tavern. I figured you ran off to see Lucinda." He comes closer, shaping his palms to my cheeks. His eyes suddenly glisten with a warning that burns all the way through me, from the back of my neck right down to my toes. "Don't ever do that again."

Part of me wants to protest at him giving me orders and seeing me like a helpless little girl. If I had my bow on me, things might not have gone so terribly wrong. But the shock of the past quarter of an hour still sits in my bones, and another, much bigger part of me is just thankful for his never-ending care. "Okay…"

He just nods, accepting that, and lets go. "You should shower now and then go to bed. It's been a long day for you."

It's been an equally long day for him, but again, I don't protest, only take off my cloak and toss it on the bed. As I head for the bathroom, he calls after me with an amused edge to his voice, "Beware of the water."

Grimacing, I twist to him. "Ice lake?"

"They don't do things by halves in this suite." Laughing, he takes off his t-shirt, heading for his own bed, and I quickly look away, hurrying to the bathroom and shutting the door. Twice in one evening would just be too much.

With the water colder than a freezer, I rush through the quickest shower of my life, clamping my chattering teeth until I'm out again and can rub myself dry and warm up a bit. Man, who builds such cruel rooms in inns? The Summer Suite—now, *that* would be a nice place to stay.

With my underwear and blouse on again for sleeping, I hurry out of the bathroom. Jack is nestled against the headboard, chest bare in this stupid, cold place, legs bent under the sheets, and Hook's map placed against his thighs. His t-shirt and jeans hang over a chair, and the red bandage is still wrapped around his arm. Because his gaze quietly follows me across the room, I pull the blouse down to cover my thighs as much as possible and hurry right over to my bed before slipping under the blanket. To hide my hot cheeks from him, I drag the comforter completely over my face, letting only my eyes peek out.

For several seconds, he looks at me in dead silence. Then he folds the map, puts it on the chest between us, and switches off the light. The sheets rustle as he scoots down and makes himself comfortable. Being a Wolf certainly has its advantages. He doesn't appear to freeze his butt off in this darn place.

I, on the other hand, couldn't curl up into a tighter ball if I tried. My limbs shiver as if rattled by an earthquake. Squeezing my eyes shut doesn't keep the cold out either. I can't even think. The crystalized air in the room numbs my brains to complete uselessness. Dang, this is going to be one long, cold night. I want back in my bed in my snug little cottage.

Minutes pass, and things don't heat up beneath my covers. Fabulous. Would anybody mind if we burned some furniture to make a cozy fire?

"Riley…" Jack's whisper drifts to me in the dark.

"Hm?"

"Don't freak out now, okay?"

Holy reindeer ride, what kind of stupid conversation

opener is that? It alone makes me think of fifty different reasons why I should go into hysterics. Rats, bugs, more snow… Icicles from my nose.

My covers lift, and he slips into my bed.

"Jack! What—"

"I could hear your teeth clattering over *there*."

The cold utterly forgotten, I stiffen in total shock.

"No bad intentions, I swear," he says quietly but with stern insistence. "I just came to warm you up. If you tell me to leave, I will."

Leave! Leave! Leave! Leave! Leave!

His arm carefully lays over me and, oh my Goodness, he's so warm! Since his face is right in front of me on the pillow, I can see the question in his eyes. And even though it would be a thousand times wiser to shove him off the bed, I don't.

My teeth still rattle a funky rhythm as he pulls me closer. Oh, burning Heaven, Jack feels like a biscuit just pulled from the oven.

His hold tightens tentatively. "Is that all ri—"

He doesn't get a chance to finish since I'm already wrapping myself around him with my arms and legs like octopus tentacles clinging to its prey. Every little inch of me wants to suck the warmth right out of Jack's naked skin.

Jack's laugh softens the darkness. "Shit, you *are* cold."

I don't care. "Too late. You came, now deal with me." Burying my face against his chest, the stutter finally eases from my breath. Nothing has ever felt better than warm Jack in my bed.

His arms gently wrapped around me, he runs his fingers through my hair. "I don't mind dealing with you, honeydrop."

While his body does wonders to my frozen limbs, his words warm me from the inside.

For a long time, we just lie there, silently tangled with each other. Jack's breathing is calm and soothing, brushing my bangs in steady intervals. The same intimacy that I noticed this morning when I was cradled on his lap creeps back into me. Even though we've never done anything even remotely close to this, nothing seems at all weird about this moment. His nearness is strangely the closest thing to home I've ever felt.

All of a sudden, a mysterious thought flickers in my mind, like a flash of light. Could it be that we played our story wrong the entire time? What if there was always meant to be more for us?

I begin to run the idea in every possible direction, but nothing seems to make sense. Eventually, I whisper his name against his skin, and he responds with a quiet, "Yeah?"

"How do you feel?"

"As long as you don't move, I should be fine," he rasps.

"Oh." What an odd answer. Sounds like he doesn't enjoy dealing with frostbitten me so much, after all. "But that's not what I meant. I'm talking about our tale. Can you feel the call of the story again or is Dr. Jekyll's serum still working?"

He takes a long time to answer, as though he needs to explore his emotions first, and then he doesn't sound exactly convincing. "I'm good."

I hug him a little tighter because I don't want him to feel bad. I never wanted that in all the years. Every time the Huntsman came with his big knife, I had to look away because it broke my heart. And then I was just happy when our next story began, and Jack was all right again, flirting and smirking like he always did.

All of that seems light years away.

"You know what's strange?" The words come out hoarse from my constricted throat. "I haven't felt the call of our story since the ball night."

Jack starts running his fingertips in circles on the back of my neck. "Since you kissed the prince?"

"Mm-hmm. I think something happened then."

His fingers anchor in my hair, his voice a mere whisper. "Did you break up with me?"

I don't answer that because I simply don't know what to say.

Chapter 10

Jack

Riley finally falls asleep in my arms, still clinging to me like a spider monkey. Her soft breaths blow against my chest in an even rhythm, warming the spot. My hand's still tangled in her hair, and I draw in the sweet smell of her skin.

What the hell am I going to do?

I swallow hard. The news of this ominous Alexander the Great dwelling in the Snow Plains completely ruined my plans. I picked that part of Fairyland for my disguise for one reason only—because I didn't think there was a real kingdom in the Marble Mountains, so I wasn't afraid that anybody would mistake Jacob for someone else. Not even Phillip knew of a king up there when I checked with him. Alex's tale must either be eons old or entirely new—just recently created by the Neverwind. Whichever it is, if he's lonely in his snow world and finds Riley on his doorstep, he'll probably welcome her with arms wide-open.

Will she give him a chance, even if he isn't Jacob—and break her promise of coming back to be just *us* again?

Honestly, judging by the struggles she went through the past week, I can barely see how she won't. Whether prince or king, to her, marrying a royal means a chance at a new ever after, and that's what she truly wants. Before she fell asleep, she basically told me that our story is over for her. She doesn't have to answer my question for me to know. I felt the shift in our tale, too, when we kissed. The crack that changed everything. Nothing will ever be the same again, no matter how hard I try. Riley gave me up. At this point, I just don't know how to keep her anymore.

Perhaps it is time to stop fighting.

A painful sigh escapes me through a raspy throat, ruffling her locks. The lie I told her the day I became her prince only entrenched me deeper in ogre shit. There was a moment or two when I could have told her the truth, and she might have forgiven me after some time. Right before she clicked Dorothy's shoes would have been the best time. Now, I have no idea how to get myself out of this clusterfuck anymore. At least not in a way that'll stop me from losing Red Riding Hood.

Are we over?

I'm exhausted. It feels like the only thing left to save us now—to save our friendship—is to let her go. After all, I'd rather see her happy in the Snow Plains than depressed by my side for the rest of her life. I'll find another tale…with Peter or the three little pigs. Maybe I can even do a holiday replacement for Russel Fang sometimes and play with the Goat and her seven kids. They probably taste better than Granny, anyway.

But what will it be like to never again meet Riley at our spot by the signpost? To return from the Marble Mountains without her and know that she's found her happy ending with someone else? My throat constricts.

Riley heaves a deep sigh in my embrace. I tilt my head down to behold her. In all our years together, I didn't do this enough. What if how she looks—how she smells— fades from my memories one day? I'm scared.

So what do I have left with her? Two more days? Two nights to carve every bit of her into my memory to keep there forever when she's long-gone? The dimples in her cheeks when she smiles, her beautiful honey eyes, her lovely pony-snicker laugh… A noose tightens around my heart, cutting like barbed wire.

I could tell her the truth in the morning, get it over and done with. Oh man, she will be so mad… She won't even let me escort her to the Snow Plains any longer, I know it. She'll just run off on her own. Not a good idea. After the incident with the Ali Baba's rat pack this evening,

I don't want her going anywhere by herself in this dangerous part of the country. She's a feisty, smart girl, but even armed with her bow, she could get hurt with the kind of ruffians that loiter around here. Thinking about her wandering through the Frosty Summits for two whole days without someone to watch over her… I grimace. An Arabian gang of thieves is bullshit compared to her falling into a crevasse. Or getting caught in a snowstorm. Who's gonna keep her warm then, huh?

No…I can't tell her the truth before we reach King Alexander's castle. She needs a protector. Once she's safe, and it's time for our farewell, I'll tell her everything about Prince Jacob—and go to hell for it. It probably serves me right for being the big, bad Wolf. I should have known not to play with an innocent heart.

"I'll miss you, honeydrop," I whisper in the cold darkness, hugging her tighter and closing my eyes.

*

Tender fingers in my fur call me back from the land of dreams. Ah, the Wolf then. How in the world did that happen? Riley's arm is draped across the back of my furry neck like I'm her teddy bear.

Lying flat on my stomach with my head resting on my paws, I open my eyes. As if she's been waiting for that, she smiles at me, still stroking the spot behind my ear. "Good morning, puppy dog."

What a nice view to wake up to. I will myself back into human form and send her a playfully scolding look from behind the crook of my elbow. "Did you change me into the Wolf?"

"You popped shape when I touched you. Just there…" She tickles my skin and grins, as if hoping for it to happen again.

I make a wry face. "Yeah, I've got myself under control when I'm awake." Even though it's a hell of a good feeling when she does that. Rolling onto my back, I scoot up against the headboard and fold my hands over my stomach on top of the blanket. "Did you sleep well?"

Riley nods. "Very." She flops onto her front and braces herself on her elbows, gazing up at me. The sun shines on her face and makes her squint then sneeze.

I nudge her nose. "Looks like the winter is just a nocturnal phenomenon in this suite." The temperature is fairly comfortable now. Riley's warm legs against mine are proof that I'm not the only one feeling it.

"Mm-hmm." A taunting beam settles in her eyes. "We should stay the day in here and leave before the night. Maybe even finish our game of pool."

My smile slowly falling, I blink at her and then swallow. Damn, I'd love nothing more than that, but it was only a joke from her end. And we shouldn't put off the inevitable any longer. After several long seconds, the gleam in her eyes seeps away, too. I slide out of bed and step into my jeans, avoiding her gaze. "You should get ready. It's a long ascent to the Frosty Summits.

Since she remains quiet while I slip on my t-shirt, I finally turn around to face her. Riley still lies in the exact same position, her lips compressed.

"What?" I snap, loosening the knot of the bandage around my left arm and tossing the strip onto the chest between the beds. "I thought you wanted to get to your king as fast as possible."

A moment of dead silence passes between us as we just stare into each other's eyes. Then she climbs out of bed, grabs her cloak, stalks to the bathroom where she left her dress last night, and slams the door shut.

Fuck, I didn't mean for that to come out so harsh. It was just...*ugh*. I bang my head against the door. These are going to be two tough days.

As I slip on my shoes and leather jacket, my glance snags on the red strip of cloth on the chest. I lower to the bedside and reach for it. Elbows resting on my thighs, I run the fabric through my fingers. Just what am I doing here...?

The bathroom door opens, making my head tilt up. Red Riding Hood walks out. She's pulled the hood low over her forehead so only her eyes flash out. For the length of a breath, she stops in the middle of the room. Our gazes lock. My heart beats loudly and painfully. Then her glance lowers, and she heads for the door. "Let's go."

I rise and, slinging the backpack over my shoulder, follow her. The red strip from her cloak goes into my pocket.

Downstairs, we hand the room key to the innkeeper. He takes a doubloon for the night and a nice packed lunch for our journey, which disappears in the backpack. I toss another handful of silver onto the counter. "Take good care of the white mare. I should be back in a few days."

Riley's head lifts to me. I meet her insecure look with a stern face. Then I turn around and leave the tavern.

We make good time before noon, neither of us speaking. I don't know what's going on in her head, but I know if I open my damn mouth, only bullshit will come out. At this point, I'd love to tell her everything. Maybe even go on my knees and just beg for forgiveness and for her to come back home with me. Except, it's like with the rough kiss in her cottage—simply the wrong way to go. The only chance I have now of protecting myself from breaking down is to build a hard wall around me. And that's what I'm doing the entire way up the mountain…brick by brick.

I wish I could say the wall works. Unfortunately, I forgot to leave out the thoughts of coming back without Riley. It's absolute hell. Now, I'm immured with them and they don't give me rest for even two minutes.

"Jack? Can we take a break?"

At her timid voice, I halt and turn. A few steps behind me, she's standing ankle-deep in the snow, shivering, her cloak wrapped tightly around her body. My astonished gaze zooms over the area. Shit, when did we reach the snowy landscape? With my forging on so doggedly, I wasn't even aware of the cold increasing.

Taking a deep breath, I nod, and we find a couple of rocks beside the path to sit on. Still silent, we eat a few of the sandwiches, and I hand her the water bottle to drink first. When we're done and everything is packed away again, I rise, ready to hike on, but Riley remains sitting. Her face is distorted in pain. "My feet hurt."

My gaze zeroes in on the peaks of the mountains. It's still a few hours' march up to the part the innkeeper pointed out to us as the last place to rest. If we don't continue now, we won't reach it before darkness falls.

I glance back at an exhausted Riley, take her hand, and gently pull her to her feet. "Come on, we can't stay here. If we don't find a place to make a fire before the night, we're going to freeze to death."

Swallowing hard, Riley nods. I let go of her hand…but she doesn't let go of mine. My gaze falls down to her squeezing fingers, and my heart constricts. A deep sigh leaves me as I meet her hopeful eyes. Then my hand tightens around hers, and we walk on.

In the morning, as we traveled, we didn't talk for obvious reasons. Now, it's because we both need all our breath to make it up the mountain. Twilight brings a bloody cold with it that bites my skin and turns Riley's cheeks and nose a deep red.

"Is it still far?" she croaks. They're the first words I've heard from her since lunch.

"No. This is the last steep incline. Behind those hilltops should be the reindeer shelter the innkeeper mentioned. There, we can rest."

As darkness swallows the mountains and a sea of stars appear in the firmament, I pull her along because it seems as if she's going to fall asleep any second even while walking. A few minutes later, we're finally there.

At the edge of the rough ascent and in the blistering cold of the night lies an acre of strangely illuminated meadow with reindeer sporadically grazing, some resting, and some eating from a monstrous pile of hay. Not far from the stack burns a purple bonfire, the flames sparkling in the night like rippling pixy glitter. Riley sucks in a sharp breath of surprise at the beautiful view. "Is that a witchfire?"

"I don't know." I've heard of the magical fires that, once kindled by the fae, burn forever until a counterspell extinguishes them. But I never came across one, and legends aren't always true in Fairyland. This one, however, seems to be.

As we step out of the snow onto the soft grassland, the frosty chill falls away from my skin. It's as if the witchfire casts a dome of protection around this place, keeping out the cold and filling the air with the warm feeling of hot chocolate in your tummy.

Riley draws closer to the fire and rubs her hands above the purple flames. Slowly, I follow her, my heart getting heavier again with every step forward, in spite of the peaceful surroundings.

So this is where we'll spend our last night together.

Chapter 11

What a lovely, magical place! I've never seen a real witchfire before, only imagined it to be fantastic when people talked about the fae supposedly casting spells on cedar wood to make it burn for all eternity. In truth, it's a thousand times more beautiful than my imagination. With all the snow around us, the sudden smell of crisp grass and hay brings a whiff of nostalgia—of home. It makes me long for the forest and my cozy cottage, having hot chocolate in front of a crackling fire…on the floor, nestled on the bear rug with Jack.

When my fingers are warm, and the icy sting has eased from my cheeks, I wander around the place, testing the edges. Outside the bewitched circle of grass, there's still the cold wind wafting over the snow-covered ground, but in the night, one can't see farther than a couple of feet. The infamous Snow Plains should be behind this barrier of darkness. Turning around, I find Jack sitting on a log near the purple, sparkling fire. He unpacks what we have left from lunch and holds out a roast turkey sandwich to me. Hungry from the long travels up here, and my tired feet cramping in my boots, I cross the meadow and lower beside him, starting to eat.

"I wonder what the place looks like," I murmur as I finish my snack because Jack is still so quiet that it makes me uncomfortable.

He crumples up the wrap of his sandwich and throws it into the fire. "The Snow Plains?" The paper goes up in pink and blue flames before it poofs into a lilac mist.

"Mm-hmm. Do you think they are as beautiful as everybody believes?"

From the backpack, he pulls the canteen and takes a draught then wipes his mouth with the back of his hand, passing the bottle on to me. "Well…I guess we'll find out tomorrow."

Reluctantly, I take it, meeting his closed expression as he stands up and then walks to the stack of hay, arranging it into a camp bed for the night. My own paper wrapping goes up in sparkly flames before I rise and silently follow him.

Jack lies down on his back, arms folded behind his head, and ankles crossed, studying the sky. With a couple of feet separating us, I curl up into a ball and watch his face. Even though it's fairly warm out here with us so close to the witchfire, the chill of loneliness creeps into my bones and makes my body tremble as though we were still sleeping in the Winter Suite.

"Jack?" I whisper.

His head tilts to me, his eyes blinking slowly in the purple glow. I swallow, and without a word, he stretches out his arm. At the silent invitation, I crawl closer and nestle against him. Gently, he folds his arm around me and tucks me to his side.

Snowdrops…

I breathe in deeply. Over the past few days, my heart always beat a bit faster when I thought of Jacob and the sweet night we spent together in the castle garden—and at the prospect of seeing him again very soon.

But I love snowdrops.

With my head resting on Jack's shoulder, I watch the beautifully illuminated night sky as the moon takes a leisurely stroll above us. When a single, glowing star falls from the firmament, a sigh escapes me because I don't dare to make a wish.

What is happening with me? Why does my chest get tighter and tighter the closer we get to the place of my definitely perfect ever after? Where has the excitement gone that gripped me after I woke up in Dorothy's house and knew where I had to go to find my true love?

"Friendships," Jack whispers, breaking softly into my thoughts.

I sniff. "What?"

"You once asked me what I wish for when I see a shooting star. I always wish to never lose my friends, for they are the only family I have."

A twinge of pain pierces my chest because I remember when I asked him about it—in Phillip's dungeon, when Jack was suffering so badly from the denied call of our story that he couldn't keep the Wolf under control. Even though it was less a question and rather a realization of just how little I knew about him after all our time together.

"Did you wish for it now, too?"

He hesitates for a long moment, his gaze still fastened on the night sky. Then finally, he tells me in a hoarse voice, "No."

My gaze switches to his face, but he still refuses to look at me. "What did you wish for?"

"I wished I could get a glimpse into your head whenever you cuddle up to me like this and sigh." His arm tightens around me ever so slightly, and his voice softens even more. "I wished I could see our story through your eyes."

If my chin wasn't resting on his chest, it would probably drop. After three long breaths, I nestle against him once more and look up into the sea of stars. "What would *I* see if I looked at the story through *your* eyes?"

For a long time, his chest lifts and falls in a quiet rhythm. He has me believing that he's not going to answer at all, when he suddenly dips his head, and I look up to meet his gaze. "You would see a most amazing girl struggling to find her place in a greater tale."

His sad look pierces my heart in a strange way, making my voice come out croaky. "And how would I *feel* looking at that girl?"

Jack swallows. "Torn… You would want her for yourself. But more than anything, you'd want her to find happiness."

Staring into his dark, mesmerizing eyes, I suddenly wonder what true happiness really feels like. What it looks like. And what it does to someone when they finally find it. I'm not sure if I ever want Jack to let me go again.

"What do *you* wish for when you see a shooting star?" he asks so quietly then, I think I can hear the moon breathe above us.

I close my eyes. "I think I've made too many wishes in the past two weeks." Too many thoughtless ones anyway. Is it a mistake to trade everything—my life, my friends, my home—for romance with a stranger in a cold place I've never been before? For the first time since I stopped being Red Riding Hood in our tale, the thought of what lies ahead scares me. My fingers claw deeper into Jack's t-shirt underneath his open leather jacket.

And suddenly, his warm hand wraps around mine.

When my eyes blink open again, he still looks at me the same way. Caring and longing…

A lump grows in my throat because I want to hold him and care for him as much he cares for me. "I don't know anymore what's left to wish for," I whisper instead of revealing my confusion.

Hesitantly, I spread my fingers so his fall between mine, and he squeezes. His other hand slides from my shoulder and slips to my neck underneath my hair. Gently, he tugs me closer, tilting his head a little more, and his gaze drops to my mouth. As he presses his lips to mine, a single tear burns in my eye and trails down my cheek. His mouth is incredibly tender, his kiss long and slow. But instead of kissing him back, a sob breaks from my throat.

I don't want him to see me so weak and vulnerable. Broken… Clenching my teeth and biting back another snivel, I turn my face away.

Without a word, Jack wraps both his arms lovingly around me and hugs me closer, resting his chin on my head. My lonely tear seeps into his t-shirt where it gets lost in the soft smell of snowdrops and moss.

What do I feel for him? I can't name it. I only know the sense of belonging is overwhelming whenever we are together like this. Could it be just another kind of love? One that is based on intimacy rather than belly butterflies?

Prince Jacob made my heart skitter with nervousness when he held me.

Jack Wolf makes it beat strong with comfort.

Inhaling deeply, I close my eyes. The sound of his pounding heart and the crackling witchfire lure me to sleep while dreams of home sweep me away.

*

At the break of daylight, I wake up and immediately miss the snugness of being held through the night. My cloak is tucked around me to keep me warm, but cold panic floods me anyway when I find the spot beside me empty. I jerk up. Where is he? He wouldn't have gone back and left me behind to meet my new ending alone, would he?

Whipping around madly, I freeze as a spiky shock of relief captures me. Jack is sitting on the log by the fire, elbows braced on his knees, staring at something red that he runs through his fingers. My heart takes a moment to calm again. The morning has barely crept over the hilltops—how long has he been sitting there?

Quietly, I climb off the hay and walk over, lowering next to him. "Hey…"

Lips compressed, he briefly turns his head my way and greets me with only a tilt of his eyebrows.

I place my hands on the wood on either side of my hips and sigh. Things aren't exactly easier today. My attention falls to his moving fingers, and I'm amazed to find the red thing there is the strip I ripped from my cloak to bind his wound in the alley behind *The Copper Gauntlet*. My eyebrows tip together. "You kept that?" I thought he'd tossed it away the morning we left the tavern.

Jack doesn't respond, only stops playing with the material and rolls it up into a ball in his palm. When he squeezes it, it feels like he's squeezing my heart. My chest clamps. This is probably going to be another long day without speaking.

I'm not sure if I can cope with this. There's so much going on in my head, things about us, about last night... I couldn't talk to him right after he kissed me, yet it's something I don't want to ignore. When he kissed me so hard in my house a few days ago, I was mad. I couldn't see it—couldn't understand what he meant to me after all these long years of being tied together in a story. But when he did it again last night, so gently and full of hope, he broke my heart.

"Jack..." I begin, and then all words die in my throat as I look around for the first time this morning. Holy wand of the Fairy Godmother!

The Snow Plains.

Acres and acres of glistening, snowy land stretch out in front of us just outside the protection of the witchfire's dome. The surface sparkles as if a million diamond shards have rained down, catching the light from all possible angles. Mighty trees of crystal grow from the snow, holding gem-like fruits in every size and color of the spectrum. They invite me to pluck them, even though they look hard enough to break my teeth. Ice birds nest in the branches, alongside owls with eyes so blue that the sky would go green with envy. Above it all, a beautiful rainbow arches from east to west on the faraway horizon, stealing my breath.

Full of astonishment, I whirl around to Jack and find him watching me from the corner of his eye. Instantly, my face falls because he doesn't share my enthusiasm. After our conversation last night under the stars, I understand why. I don't want to push him with my excitement about a place he must have come to hate, so I quietly stand up and walk across the meadow to the very edge of the firelight dome. There, I bend down and touch the ground. The snow here is harder than that which we walked through on our ascent. It feels like real crystal, shards of jewels sifting through my hands as I lift some of it. It's unspeakably beautiful. Everything about this place is.

But it's also cold. And alien. It's quiet up here. The birds don't sing, there's no humming of the bees from the woods, and the icy leaves don't rustle in the wind. The only sound is the ripple of the snow grains through my hands, and the munching of the reindeer chewing on the hay nearby.

I miss the song of the Wood of 1000 Dawns. And most of all, I miss hearing it with Jack.

In my vision, I can just see myself walking around the bend, watching the robins dance in a magical circle beneath the clouds right before I meet him and he offers me his one-sided smile. With a hopeful flutter in my heart, I twirl around…but there is no smile on his face now. The cold of the Snow Plains behind me creeps under my skin.

Am I ruining everything?

Ever so slowly, I walk back to the witchfire and lower beside Jack again. With my feet pulled onto the log, I loop my arms around my legs and rest my cheek on my knees, watching him for several silent seconds.

He started playing with the red strip of cloth again, his gaze focused on his hands instead of the glamorous surroundings. A muscle works his jaw.

"How do you feel?" I whisper with soft caution.

His answer is a throaty rasp. "Why do you keep asking me that?"

"Because what *I'm* feeling makes no sense to me." Biting my lip, I struggle to find the right words when tears clog my throat. "I don't understand it, and I'm hoping that maybe you do. So please, Jack, tell me…" Carefully, I reach out to touch his hand. "How do you feel?"

He lets my fingers brush along his, watching my every move. His skin is cold this morning, much colder than my own, so I slide from the log and kneel on the ground in front of him, covering both of his hands with mine. Jack stares into my eyes for an endless moment until, finally, one single word wrenches out from him. "Helpless."

The ground sways beneath me at the sheer impact of his pain. I feel as if I'm losing myself in the quake.

Jack laces our fingers, squeezing so tightly that he cuts off my blood flow. "There are so many things I should tell you, but I can't because, over there, behind that crystal landscape"—his gaze briefly wanders to the spot where I stood a minute ago—"lies what you dream of. I don't want to stand in your way, Riley. But I can't turn around, either. And I simply hate that you've forced me to come along and deliver you to the doorstep of a king who will replace me at your side." The last words are no more than a hoarse whisper.

It sounds as if he's met a dead end. But not only him. With a closed throat, I turn around to glance at the Snow Plains…and I don't see a future for me there. No love. No happily ever after. Suddenly, a very clear picture of happiness appears before me. And it has the eyes of a Wolf.

It happened in recurring moments, when Jack chased me up the stairs of the mill, and we jumped down into the hay together. When he tried to sniff out the apple I was hiding inside my cloak after I let him out of Phillip's dungeon, and we strolled through the woods. When he slipped into my bed in the Winter Suite and tucked me against him to warm me through the night. And most of all, when I thought I lost him in the fight with the two thieves and he came limping out of the shadows.

My every happy moment in the past two weeks was somehow tied to Jack. I don't want to give him up, not for anything in this fairy world, and certainly not for a prince in a cold kingdom. So when I turn back to him and find his eyes, I abandon all the stupid wishes I've made and quietly ask, "Can we go home now?"

He freezes. His gaze nails me, his fingers tight like

manacles around my hands. Then his brows quirk the smallest bit. "What?"

"I want to go home."

I can feel the battle inside him when he forces himself to release me. Gently, he strokes a lock behind my ear, while his face is still taut with fear. "But your happy ending is waiting over there."

"No, it's not." My voice almost breaks as I shake my head. "I don't want adventure anymore. No prince. Please, Jack, let's just go back home and be Red Riding Hood and the Wolf again. I love our story. I love the forest. I love everyone who lives there, and…" *You.* The word lingers between us.

His hand slips behind my neck, and he dips his forehead against mine, his expression still torn. "Are you sure?"

With determination, I stare at his closed eyes and nod. Then I rise and, taking his hands once more, I pull him up with me.

"And you won't change your mind on the way home?" he croaks.

I shake my head.

"Or when we're back in the forest?"

Smiling, I shake my head again and don't break eye contact as I bend down to pick up the backpack. Slipping my arms through the straps, I reach for his hand again and then drag him with me…away from the witchfire…away from the Snow Plains…in the direction of home.

Chapter 12

Jack

Everything feels strange as we leave the Frosty Summits. The restrained smile Riley gives me when I slide the backpack off her shoulders and sling it over my own tries hard to convince me the painful journey is really over. We're going home now, and it will be just *us* again. But a splintered part of my heart doesn't dare trust the peace. What if this is just for today? If she already has a new plan to change her ever after tomorrow? Let's face it, she's been erratic about her ideas before.

Merely her petite hand slipping into mine and firmly

holding on makes me follow her down any path she goes. I can't take my eyes off her, for what if I miss the moment when her decision skips in another direction again?

And of course, there's still the untold truth about Jacob.

I intended to tell her everything once we reached King Alexander's castle. Since we're no longer heading there, is now the right time? I know I can't put it off too much longer, but every time Riley looks at me, and I want to speak past the lump lodged in my throat, a terrible fear takes hold that I'll lose her beautiful smile again. No matter how often I tried in the past half hour, no sound moves past my lips.

"I don't like it when you're so quiet," she murmurs, casting a wary glance at me.

I wish I wasn't. But guilt has my lips sealed. "Sorry."

Riley's hand slips from mine. She stops and squats on the roadside to cup some snow and put it into her mouth. The water bottle was empty this morning. Judging by the satisfied moan, she was probably thirsty. Using the short break, I fetch the canteen from the backpack and hunker down to squeeze some snow through the opening. In a few minutes, it should turn into water, which we'll need for the long journey back to the Wood of 1000 Dawns.

It's strange how, when thinking of home, Riley's cottage pops into my mind first instead of my apartment in Grimmwich. The cozy fire in front of her sofa, the whimsical clock on the chest that ticks backward. When she went missing after the ball, and I was lying on her porch waiting for her, the place gave me a sense of a peace I desperately needed—something I took comfort in.

"Jack?"

At her voice, I look up, and a snowball hits me straight on the forehead. *What the—?* All former thoughts scatter, and I shake the snow out of my hair. From the corner of my eye, I see that she's already rolling another one.

"Drop it," I growl through a smirk.

"Or else?" Grinning, Riley hauls her arm back, ready to fling it at me. "Does the big, bad Wolf come out to play?"

She asked for it. Leaving the canteen on the ground, I slowly rise and then blow her down with a quick, hard wolf-breath. She flies backward into the soft snow and giggles, tossing the ball anyway—it lands heaven only knows where.

Turning into the Wolf, I prowl closer until I stand right above her, and blow a breath into her face that makes her hair fly. She squeezes her eyes shut for a moment and laughs. When she blinks them open again, her look is way too soft. It instinctively makes me change back into myself before she comes up with the idea of rubbing behind my ear. Kneeling over her with my hands braced in the cold snow, I lean down until our noses touch. "You should never tempt a wicked Wolf, honeydrop."

"You know what?" Her snicker eases into a soft smile. "I don't think you're half as mean as you always try to make me believe."

Her words slice through my heart. She doesn't know what she's saying because she hasn't heard the truth yet. I hesitate for a moment before I rasp, "What if you're wrong? And I'm really the bad guy?"

Her good-humored gaze doesn't waver from mine as her palms lay feather-light against my chest. "I'll risk it."

A snug wave of sweet warmth rolls through me. I didn't quite know what to make of her words back at the meadow by the witchfire, but this sounds very much like approval. Doesn't it? A suggestion to try the *us* thing? My heart steps up a beat, and I swallow. "Are you sure?" My gaze drops to her lips before I tilt my head and whisper against them, "Because there's no going back if you say yes."

And then I kiss her…cautiously, always giving her the chance to escape if she wants to, like she did last night in the hay. Relief fills me that she doesn't break into sobs this time. Instead, her hands come around my neck, and she moves her lips shyly against mine.

One little kiss…two… It feels as if she's actually made a decision about us. She'll no longer run to the end of Fairyland to find someone else. A thrill rushes over my skin, similar to the anticipation of a hunt, as if I've been chasing this little deer through the forest forever.

When she opens her mouth for me, I deepen the kiss. Her tongue is cold from the snow she sucked, but it warms quickly against mine as I begin to stroke it. Tender, slow licks to seduce the fawn out of her hiding and coax her into surrender.

She tastes incredibly good, her ever-present smell of morning dew and wood strawberries crowding my senses. When her fingers run up my neck, and she finds the ticklish spot behind my ear again, I squeeze my eyes shut and moan against her mouth, gently nipping her bottom lip.

Riley shivers beneath me and, even though I know most of it comes from the tender assault, I don't want her to freeze in the snow. With a brush of my lips across her upper one, I bring the kiss to an end. For the length of another breath, I hover over her, looking deep into her honey eyes until they crinkle with the tiniest of smiles. Then I plant a quick kiss on the tip of her nose and rise. Taking my hand, she lets me pull her to her feet and then pats off the white sludge from her cape while I pick up the backpack and shoulder it.

"Everything okay?" I ask softly, waiting by her side.

Her cheeks lightly flushed, Riley nods, the smile not yet completely gone from her face. Gently, I stroke a snowflake out of her locks and then lean my forehead against hers. "Shall we go home now?"

"Yes, please." Tentatively, she fishes for my hand. Instantly, the melted-chocolate feeling returns to my stomach. It's unbelievable what this girl can do to me with the tiniest of things. The corners of my mouth twitching up, I lace our fingers, and together we start off.

While we took a whole day to make the ascent to the Frosty Summits, we make it down in less than half. The way home is always the shortest, they say. Seems to be true.

Back at *The Copper Gauntlet*, she cuddles Lucinda for endless minutes. It's hard to separate those two, but Riley's stomach grumbles with hunger, and I want her to eat something before we head out. So I drag her into the tavern with an arm draped around her shoulders.

In the entrance, we bump into Ali Baba and a group of his thieves. The two at the back eye us with pale faces. The wounds from my fangs on their arms are wrapped with dirty bandages. Their throats bobble with gulps as they quietly step aside to let us pass.

Heading to the same spot as last time, Riley giggles and loops her arm around mine, crowding me. "Did you see the terror in their faces?" After we lower into opposite chairs, she leans across the table. "I'm glad you didn't eat them."

They certainly deserved it, but killing characters in Fairyland is not my job. Who knows what kind of story I would have ruined if I did?

With a surprised grin, the innkeeper comes by to take our order. "That was a short visit at your prince's place," he says to Riley. "Was the king not what you were looking for then?"

Quickly, her gaze slides to me. Then she replies with absolute lack of regret, "We didn't meet him. The Marble Mountains are just too cold a place for me."

Is she serious? Even after our quick roll in the snow, I find it hard to believe that we're at the end of this adventure. But from the bright look on Riley's face, it's true.

The rotund, gray-haired man nods and makes his way into the kitchen to get our meals. A few minutes later, while Riley wolfs down her chicken filet and salad, she babbles nonstop about the Wood of 1000 Dawns and how she hopes that Granny is back home from her vacation in Bedrock. I don't get a word in. And even though a bad feeling nags at me because there's still so much to say, it's adorable to see her this high-spirited again.

"What's wrong with you?" she suddenly asks around a bite of food, scrutinizing the plate of untouched spareribs in front of me. "All you did the past fifteen minutes was shove your veggies around."

Guess, this is my cue. I put the fork aside and wipe my still clean fingers on the cloth napkin. "I'm not hungry."

"And I'm full." Laying her knife and fork down, too, she gives me that cute smile again and rises from the chair. "Let's take off."

I'm about to ask her to sit down again so I can tell her what's really on my mind, but she's already heading for the door. I have no choice but to pay for our meals and say goodbye to the innkeeper before I follow her. Riley's anticipation of finally getting home knows no end today.

If I learned one thing over the past two weeks, it's to never underestimate a girl in a red cloak once she's on a mission.

We saddle the white mare and lead her out of the stable. For the length of the cobblestoned road, Riley walks beside Lucinda, holding the reins, but as soon as we reach the borders of the town, I help her mount, and she sends me an expectant look. "Are you running as the Wolf again?"

If I do, we're home before nightfall, and that's obviously what she hopes for. So I nod and hand her the backpack, transforming while she hauls it over her shoulders. At least for the time the animal is out, I don't have to try and find the right moment to come clean with the truth. And running with the Neverwind feels extremely calming…because it's taking us home.

The horse's hooves trample the dirt on the road beside me in an ever-steady rhythm as we leave the Rhymeshire and cross the beautiful meadows of Avalon. In the late afternoon, dwarfs and elves shout "good day" at us from the beer garden of the *Teacup Pup* in Glimmergulf, and when we finally leave the last hill behind, the Wood of 1000 Dawns rises majestically before us in the golden glow of a marvelous sunset.

As soon as we cross the borders, Riley halts the white mare with a sharp pull on the reins. I change into my human self in time to help her down from the saddle and, immediately, she dashes to a mighty copper beech. Her eyes dreamily closed, she hugs the massive tree and presses her face against the trunk. "Finally."

Lucinda's reins held tightly in my hand, I inhale deeply and let the spirit of the wood swarm through me, too. The soothing scent of moss and leaves drifts up my nostrils, and in the thicket all around us, the birds sing their evening song, welcoming us home.

Even the mare begins to prance next to me, pulling hard at the reins as if seeking freedom.

"She's excited to be back," Riley says, coming back from the beech and rubbing Lucinda's forehead. "We should take her to the castle first."

"I don't think that will be necessary." I fasten the reins to the saddle and then smack the horse on her behind. "Off you go!"

In a wild gallop, she races through the trees, taking the shortest way to Castle Grove.

Turning back to me, Riley tucks her hands into the pockets of her red dress, rocking back and forth on her heels. Someone's impatient. Laughing softly, I grip the straps of the backpack on my shoulders and nod in the opposite direction of Lucinda's dust before I start walking. It's only a short hike through the woods to Riley's place.

"Tomorrow, I want to go and check if Granny is back yet," she cheers, "and then we can start playing our story again, perhaps. If you want…"

The idea is nice. There's just one catch. "Do you feel the call again?"

The hopeful beam vanishes from her face. After a deep sigh, she presses her lips together and then shakes her head.

Her gaze searches mine, and her voice drops to a quiet murmur. "Do you?"

I wish I did, but nothing tugs at the Wolf. "No."

"What does that mean?"

"Well, with me, it could just be that Dr. Jekyll's wonder elixir is still working. And with you…" I draw in a long breath, queasy doubts clenching my chest as I pull my brows together in a frown. "Perhaps, your adventure isn't over yet."

"What do you mean? I don't plan on building another prince trap." She makes a wry face. "You won't believe who slept in the other one."

"A dwarf?"

Her expression takes on an incredulous edge. "How did you know?"

I give her a sheepish grimace. "The morning before the ball, I went there to check. Since he didn't mean any danger"—for he was no prince who could replace me—"I let him sleep on."

"Oh, how very kind of you not to eat him." She rolls her eyes, and her snicker echoes from the trees. "I guess I should be glad you didn't come to the feast with me after all and rough up the *dangerous* royals there."

I swallow.

It's a sheer miracle that I was able to put the subject off for so long, but now, it feels as if we've reached the absolute end of that reprieve. Damn. The little hairs on the back of my neck begin to bristle with unease.

The signpost that always fills my chest with a small bout of excitement at first sight stands at the crossing ahead. But it doesn't affect me like that today. Instead, a heavy reluctance creeps into my steps.

Riley stops and lovingly strokes the pole, her gaze lifted to the sign pointing to Glitter Hollow. When she tilts her head to me, a bashful smile dimples her cheeks. "Would you like to…um…come home with me"—the corner of her cloak clutched in her fist, she points down the path—"and have a cup of hot chocolate together?"

"Riley…" I take two deliberate breaths, trying to calm my nervously beating heart, but it's pointless. "There's something I need to tell you."

Her arm sinks, and she blinks at me with an uneasy expression. Suddenly, the backpack feels unspeakably heavy on my shoulders. I shrug it off, dropping it to the forest floor. Then I rub my hands over my face and cut a pleading look to the sky. Shit, where do I even begin?

"Jack…?" A fearful edge underscores her voice as she narrows her eyes. "You're scaring me. What is it?"

No more stalling… I lick my lips while my chest heaves with a sigh. "I was there."

The corners of her cloak still clasped in both hands, she brings them to her heart, scrutinizing me with confusion. "There…*where?*"

"At Phillip's ball." Cautiously, I reach out to take her hand and lower my chin to look her straight in the eye. "On his birthday."

As if she's swarmed by a feeling of foreboding, her face pales, and she squeaks, "What?"

"I came there in the disguise of a…prince."

"Why didn't I see you then?"

I close my eyes, expelling a breath. "You did." Man, this is going to be tough. I clear my sandpapered throat as I look at her again. "You even danced with me."

A moment passes in complete silence, then her eyes grow to twice their size as things apparently click into place. I can almost see how her mind jumps back and forth between Jacob and Casanova. To clear all doubt, I add quietly, "And we kissed in the garden."

Riley yanks her hand out of mine, breathing fast. She stumbles a step back. I follow her and reach out, but she avoids my touch. Her mouth opens and closes several times before snapping utterly shut. Her lips are compressed, brows drawn in a hard line, and she stares at me as if she's never seen me before. Then she shakes her head. "How could you?"

There's so much hurt and betrayal in those simple words. And all I can do is plead. "Riley, please…I'm sorry."

"Sorry?" she croaks. "What kind of morbid mind games were you playing with me?"

"It wasn't a game. It was my only chance to show you that you don't need a prince to find love."

"By pretending to *be* one?" Her voice breaks at her screech as she retreats even farther from me. Her sudden yell frightens a flock of birds from the closest tree, and they flutter away. "You—you... Oh my *Goodness!*" Riley grabs her hair, her gaze darting around the place in utter horror. "Did the others know about this?"

My throat hurts when I gulp. "Phillip. And Eric. Your friends had no idea."

Her eyes stop their mad flicking and settle on me. She pants as if she's been chased through half the forest, her eyes misting. "And when were you going to tell me about this?"

Torn by emotions, I reach for her once more, needing to touch her, hoping she'll understand. "On so many occasions."

"Ah, yes, and that's why you waited until now, right?"

"What? *No!*" This is completely going down the wrong way.

She keeps stumbling backward as I follow. "Why did you even take me to the Snow Plains if it was you all along?"

Helplessly clenching my teeth, I grit out, "Riley...could you please stop walking away from me?"

"I can't believe you fooled me so terribly. What kind of sick person does that?" And then she stops so abruptly, I almost knock her over. With a wave of hope, I gently grab her upper arms, but she doesn't even seem to see me right then. Her face is frozen with terror as she stares right through me into the distance. "By all the fairy tales! The shift when we kissed—I thought it was because I changed *my* ever after. But I didn't..." Slowly, her horror-stricken gaze meets my eyes. "You changed *yours*. And you caught me up in it."

I freeze. What she says makes sense. I did feel the shift she's speaking about. Damn, the ground even quaked beneath my feet in Phil's garden. Could it really be because I cracked my own ever after by kissing the right girl?

Her eyes misty, Riley tugs at her arms, making my grip tighten around them. "You tricked me into a new ending," she says with an ice-cold edge and, with anther yank, finally tears free of my hold. "You did this on purpose. So I had no other choice but to be stuck with you!"

Panic floods me. "No."

"That's why you didn't tell me. And why you let me travel to the Marble Mountains like a fool. You were so fixated on our tale that you wouldn't let me find true love." Her voice raises more with each word. She sniffs. "So you invented someone because you knew I'd come back if that someone didn't exist."

"No! *Yes...*" My face crumples as I take her hands, pleading with her. "But that's only half of the truth."

Riley pulls away with a deadly hiss. "Don't touch me!"

Horror keeps me frozen. "Please, let me explain."

She's been fighting all this time to keep her tears at bay, but now one of them trails down her cheek. "You just did. And I don't care for more crap from you!" Her nostrils flare as if she's breathing hard through her nose. "Drop dead, Jack Wolf!"

Riley whirls around and breaks into a run. Her cloak

flies behind her, and her hard sob is the last thing carried on the wind.

A wild surge of terror rises inside me, blanking out the woods and everything around me. My chest feels as if it's been hacked in two, my heart falling right out and plunging to the forest floor.

My desperate gaze hangs on the red spot that's getting smaller and smaller beyond the line of trees until it's gone and nothing of Riley is left. Reeling back, I knock against the signpost. Every breath hurts. I slide down the pole and sit on the ground. There, I draw up my knees and bury my face in my arms.

By Grimm, what have I done?

Chapter 13

The Wood of 1000 Dawns is closing in on me. Everything is so tight, so close, I can hardly breathe. Home…I need to get home. It'll all be better once I'm home and can lock the world out. At least I keep telling myself that as I dash through the underbrush.

Harsh sobs break from my throat by the time the cottage finally appears. I storm onto the porch and through the door, closing and locking it before falling against it. But the pressing feeling doesn't go away.

Because it's not outside, it's within me.

Pain tightens my chest until my heart barely has room to beat inside. My eyes wet with tears, I summon the strength to push away from the door, stumble through the cabin, and knock into the couch. Is there nowhere I can go to escape my aching self? The clock from Alice ticks loudly on the shelf, the hands running backward as usual. If only that was really possible—to turn back time.

Steeped in my own cloud of misery, I lurch to the bed and slump down, burying my face in the pillow. Why did Jack hurt me so? I was the happiest girl when he kissed me in the snow, and it seemed as if we'd found our own happily ever after together. I was on top of the mountain with him. Then, with what he said under the signpost—with only those few words—he ruined everything!

The agony set in the moment I understood who the prince really was, and how Jack was fooling me so terribly since the night of the ball. The horror robbed me of the ground beneath my feet. I fell—from the top of the mountain down to the very bottom of an abyss.

Now I'm lying here, unable to breathe, to move, to think. I only know it's over, everything has changed, and it hurts so badly.

Because right before the end, I fell in love with Jack Wolf.

When he just played a cruel game with me so he wouldn't lose our story.

Pressing my palms against my swollen eyes to stop more tears from falling, I gulp in huge amounts of air, trying to ease my sobs. I refuse to cry any more over a cheater like him—a liar! He doesn't deserve it.

In fact, he isn't worth another thought, ever again.

*

A restless night now lies behind me. I drank seven cups of hot chocolate—at least that's what the dirty dishes in the sink say. Yet I'm pretty sure, close to morning, I had two drinks from the same mug.

Tiredness follows me everywhere, making my eyelids heavy. I just scurry around in my hut and in the garden, too fast for sleep to actually catch me. Work helps. It distracts from all the crap with Jack, so I start chopping wood at sunrise, and when every single log is split into handy pieces, I sit down on the front porch and begin gluing the broken pots of my two ficus together. The Fairy Godmother created quite a mess when she blustered onto my porch on the evening of the ball.

Carefully, I push them back into their places to the left and right of the door. They're a mosaic of a thousand shards now, but I'm quite pleased with my repair job. My robin friend seems to like the new pot style, too because he circles down from his nest under the roof onto my open palm, and I swear the corners of his little beak lift. On the other hand, maybe that's just from being happy to see me again. With the tip of my finger, I brush over his head. "I missed you, too, little fella."

Soft footsteps sound behind me as someone steps onto the porch stairs, and I jerk around. A flash of shock zips through me, my fist squeezing the robin. He screeches out in panic while I stare at Jack standing five feet away from me. It takes a stunned second before I'm able to unclamp my fingers and free the frantic bird.

He flies back to the roof and rants down from his nest in a flurry of sharp tweets, but the noise drifts in as if from faraway as I'm caught up in the sad eyes of the Wolf. Dark rings beneath them give the impression that he didn't sleep any better than I did last night.

"What do you want?" I snap, taking a wary step backward.

His gaze falls to the floorboards between us. The sleeves of his black sweatshirt pushed to the elbows, he tucks his hands into his jeans pockets, biting his bottom lip. A sigh tears from him before he looks up at me again. "Can we talk?"

Yeah, like hell. No matter how much wood I hacked this morning, I'm not yet over the bullshit deal he served me. "You can talk to the ficus." Spinning on my heels, I trudge back into the house and slam the door.

"Riley, please…" his voice drifts inside, his footfalls coming closer. "Give me a chance to explain."

My answer is the click of the lock as I turn the key.

"Come on, open the door."

"Or what?" I yell in anger. "Are you going to blow my house down?"

"Don't be ridiculous."

"Why? Isn't that what big, bad wolves do best?" Walking backward, I keep the door in my sight. "Blowing houses down…eating pigs and people…pretending to be someone they're not?"

A thud sounds on the door as if he turned and fell with his back against it. "I'm sorry, okay?"

"No, nothing is okay." Crossing my arms, I scowl, even though it's just for the door. "Now get lost before I call for Edward Scissorhands and tell him to castrate you."

Several silent seconds tick by. My nerves are pulled taut like stretched wire. Then I catch a glimpse of him through the window as he leaves my porch. After one last glance backward, he draws up his hood and, with his head hanging, shuffles away into the forest.

I slump onto the couch and groan at the ceiling, smacking my fists into the cushion beside me. "Stupid fleabag!"

An hour later, my muscles and nerves finally relax. Jack didn't come back, and for some reason, I have a feeling he won't for a while. Good. I don't want to see him again. Ever. But there's someone I *do* need to talk to.

Out in the garden, I lift my hand and call down an SMS. When the stork in a blue vest appears, ready to record my message, I cough a little and then speak loudly and clearly. "This is a message from Riley Redcoat to Princess Cindy. Hey! Can you meet me at Rory's? It's urgent." My voice is none too gentle and, with a nod, I signal that the bird can fly off and deliver the text.

Because Princess Cinderella and Aurora are neighbors, she'll be there in a few minutes while for me on foot, it takes over half an hour to get to Castle Grove. I grab my cloak from the armrest of the floral wingback chair and wrap it around my shoulders, clasping the button at the collar. Outside, I toss a handful of grains onto the porch rail for my robin friend as an apology for the squeeze attack earlier, and then I head off.

The Wood of 1000 Dawns is quiet today, as if all the birds and squirrels are still asleep. No matter which direction I turn, there's no pair of eyes blinking back at me like they usually do from all possible places. The small hairs on my forearms rise at the eerie silence. I pull my hood lower down my forehead and scurry on.

Eventually reaching Rory's castle, I cross the bridge over the moat. The bang of the brass knocker on the wood echoes inside.

"Coming…" Phillip's voice reaches me from behind the door shortly before the lock rattles, and he opens. "Riley!" His face brightens with a welcoming smile. "I was wondering if you two were back when I saw Lucinda in the stables this morning."

He can act as friendly as Bambi all he wants. I, on the other hand, clench my teeth so hard I think my molars might crack. Is there steam coming from my nose, too?

Phillip reads all the signs of acute danger perfectly right and falls silent, even taking a wary step back.

Shamefully, he lowers his head and murmurs, "The girls are on the patio." Then he quickly steps aside and lets me in.

I nail him with another grim glare as I stride through the door and across the entrance hall to the garden.

Aurora is seated on a cushioned chair by a marvelously decked-out brunch table. Her leg with the cast rests on the stool next to her. Nearby, Cindy sways back and forth on the porch swing, her dirty, ragged dress swishing around her calves. The SMS must have caught her at the beginning of her tale with the old hag and the stepsisters.

"You escaped from your story?" I ask instead of a greeting, and both their heads snap around.

Instantly, Cindy is on her feet and hugs me. "You said it was urgent. Of course, I did."

"Well then, I don't want to hold you up too long." Gently, I push away from her and take a seat across from Aurora, waiting for Cindy to sit down, too. With my elbows braced on the round table, I lean forward. "Did you guys know what was going on at the ball? About Jacob?"

Rory sends me a smile, stirring her tea with a silver spoon. "Sure. You two had a very nice time in the garden, and the past few days, you were off meeting him in the Snow Plains."

"So you really didn't know what the guys were up to?" My pleading gaze nails them both. I just need to know if my friends were in on this or not. But from their baffled stares, I get the feeling that Jack told me the truth...for once.

Cindy's forehead creases with lines of worry. "What's the matter?"

In a ninety-second rush and with barely a pause for breath, I tell them why I *didn't* meet Prince Jacob—or rather, how I came to know that I was actually traveling *with* him through the country all along.

Rory's face pales with every word I spew out, and when she learns that her charming husband was in on the wicked plot from the beginning, the teacup shatters in her hands. "Darling?!" she forces through gritted teeth, glancing at the open French doors.

Instead of her husband, Edgar appears on the patio. With his hands clasped behind his back, he bows to Aurora. "Milady, Prince Phillip asked me to inform you that he has packed his suitcase and left the country. He expects to return in a year or two." His apologetic gaze slides to me. "Or when the apocalypse is over."

Rory flings the handle and what little of the cup is still attached to it toward the castle. "Phillip! Don't be silly. Come out now, you coward!"

A figure appears in the shadows. Stepping forward, Phillip ducks his head and looks at us from under his lashes. "I'm sorry," he murmurs.

"What in the world were you thinking, helping Jack fool Riley like that?"

Cautiously, he heads toward us, his gaze finding mine instead of his wife's. "I thought I'd help a friend get the girl he loves."

Leaning back in the chair, I cross my arms and grunt. "We both know that Jack's reasons for it were quite shady."

"*I* know why he did it." Speaking with a little more insistence, Phillip lowers into the chair that Aurora freed for him by taking her leg down. "But I doubt *you* do."

Cindy supports me while pointing a spoon at Phillip, "It certainly had nothing to do with *love,* or he wouldn't have behaved so terribly and lied to her."

His gaze darts to her and then comes back to me. "Did Jack tell you what he did for you before the ball?" When my face remains hard and my lips stay sealed, he sends me a sad smile. "You didn't give him a chance to explain, did you?" A sigh leaves him. "To be the prince you wanted, he went through quite the torture. He let us pop painful things into his eyes to make them blue and, damn, Riley, he even ate chalk."

Rory's eyes grow wide, and she stiffens next to him. "Chalk?" she croaks in shock.

"He was hiding behind the bar when you came into the room the afternoon before the ball," Phillip says with a resigned expression. Judging by the way she claps her hands over her mouth, it probably makes sense to her, but neither of them is going to explain.

"Ugh." Grimacing, Cindy snags a croissant from the plate in the middle and starts plucking it to pieces. "Eating chalk sounds nasty."

My face scrunches, too. "Who would do such a stupid

thing?"

"A Wolf in love." Phillip laughs softly, then his face sobers again. "When you disappeared to Kansas, he went completely out of his mind. He didn't rest for a minute, roaming the forest and town day and night." He tilts his head, and the noon sun softens his blue eyes. "Maybe you should give him a chance to tell you the whole story. You can still decide if you want to hate him afterward." From across the table, he gives me a hopeful grin, holding out a white jug to me. "Hot chocolate?"

My stomach churns.

*

After the frustrating visit at Castle Grove, instead of going home, I take a right turn to Granny's house. My head swarms with everything Philip told me, and I don't want to become maudlin on my couch with too many thoughts gnawing at me. Besides, I haven't seen her in a while, and I want to make sure she's all right and back from her vacation.

My gaze fastened on the forest floor in front of me, I shuffle along the narrow path through the trees. Birds sing a merry song in the branches now, but the closer I get to the place where Granny lives, the quieter everything becomes again. Goosebumps creep over my skin. I wrap my cloak tighter around me, kicking a stone along the way, and take the last bend to the small cottage.

The next instant, two familiar voices drift to me. My chin snaps up, and I freeze in shock. My grandmother stands on the doorstep, dressed in her finest turquoise coat and skirt, her salt-and-pepper hair pulled into a tight bun at the back of her head. The fluffy pink slippers she wears are a total fail in matching her clothes.

And with her is Jack. From the way it looks, they're saying goodbye. Of course, the forest would be silent when the Wolf is around.

Granny shapes her palms to his cheeks and smiles up into his face like she often did with me when I came to her with a bruised knee or cuts on my arms after sneaking through the underbrush. "You're a good boy," she tells him, blinking her old eyes. Then they find me over his shoulder, and her smile grows just a tiny bit wider.

Tracing the direction of her look, Jack slowly turns around, and my gran's hands slip away from his face. Instead of smiling, he swallows when he sees me, and I clench my teeth. "Goodbye, Granny," he murmurs, his voice so low it's barely louder than a fox's sigh. But he doesn't look back at her because his gaze holds mine captive.

As he heads toward me on the narrow stone path winding through the front garden, I start walking, too. My heart begins to pound loudly in my chest with Phillip's words ringing in my ears. *"Damn, Riley, he even ate chalk."* I can't hold Jack's stare any longer and lower my gaze just before our shoulders brush as we pass each other.

Something red on his wrist catches my eye. It wasn't there this morning. But Jack quickly pulls down the sleeve of his black hoodie and hides whatever it is. I don't look back but hurry to Granny, kiss her briefly on the cheek, and then make my way into the house, glad when she closes the door.

Two empty teacups are on the table, plus two plates, one with only crumbs, and the other holding an untouched piece of cake. Granny always eats hers, so I guess Jack wasn't hungry when he came for a visit.

"How was Bedrock?" I busy myself in the kitchen. For some reason, I can't bring myself to turn around and meet my grandmother's eyes. The kettle above the fire is still half full. With a dishcloth wrapped around the handle, I take it to the counter and pour myself a cup of tea.

"Lovely. You need to come with me one day and try that running car. It's fantastic."

Leave the Wood of 1000 Dawns again? I don't think I really want to. "Yeah, maybe."

When Granny joins me in the kitchen, she pulls the sheer curtains away from the window in front of me. I cast a cautious glance out while dipping a raspberry-flavored teabag into the hot water. But Jack has already disappeared into the shadowy woods.

"What did he want?" I murmur, my voice hard, my flat gaze back on the tea.

"He came to apologize for making me unemployed."

"Yeah, about that..." I slide a quick glance at her. "I'm

sorry."

Granny brushes my cheek with her knuckles. "Don't worry, dear child. I'm old. It's okay to go into retirement." She snickers. "Less getting eaten, more time for other things."

I wonder what those *things* might be, considering she's wearing such a fine outfit today. Applying for another job, perhaps?

She picks up the kettle and fills another cup at the table. "Besides, Jack also told me his side of the story."

Grasping my cup in both hands, I turn around to lean against the counter behind me and blow into the steaming beverage. "Then I hope it was an entertaining afternoon for you."

Without a word, she offers me a seat and pulls out the chair that Jack must have used with the empty cup and the full plate still in front. I rather remain by the counter and watch her sit down at the head of the table than sit where he did. While she spoons four heaps of sugar into her black tea and stirs, her expression becomes contemplative. "It was a beautiful tale," she murmurs, putting the spoon down. "I think you would have enjoyed it, too."

Grunting a snort, I lower my cup. "What is it with everyone wanting me to listen to him today?"

Granny's face splits with a grin as she reaches out and pats the table with the cake waiting. I push away from the counter and stalk over, but I lower into another chair, hopefully making my point clear.

Obviously, I don't because she just pushes the plate across the table right in front of me, her smile never wavering. "Would you like to tell me your side of the story now?"

"What for? It's not a whole lot different from what he probably told you."

"Really?" Her eyes grow big with perfectly faked wonder. "Then I don't understand what you're still doing here instead of running to Jack and flinging your arms around his neck."

"I know that you always liked him a lot, but this is ridiculous." I pick up the fork and skewer the corner of the piece of chocolate fudge cake. "He's a cheater. Didn't you read that between his lines?" Angry, I shove a bite into my mouth.

Several quiet seconds turn into a solid minute as she just studies me, probably trying to figure out the best words to change my mind. But she won't be lucky. There's no rub in my view. This time, she'll lose because Jack is a dork. Casting an extremely innocent look at the ceiling, she finally mumbles, "Cheater, hm..." When her gaze drops back to me, she scratches her chin. "And you don't think that shooting a king with a magical arrow from Cupid's tree to make him fall in love with you could be called...well...cheating, too?"

Darn her!

I sip from my tea, glaring at her over the rim of the cup. "It's not the same."

"Because he is a Wolf and you're nice little Red Riding Hood, yes, I understand." She gulps her hyper-sweet tea then puts the cup down, sending me a self-satisfied smirk.

"Granny!" I whine because I hate it when she pours her sarcasm on me. A good old lady like her shouldn't even know that kind of irony. "Is there actually any helpful advice you have to aid me with my problem?"

"Yes."

"And that is?"

She pats my hand. "Glass houses. Stones. I think you know the story."

Snorting, I roll my eyes. "You're so funny today."

"Really? Oh, good." She giggles and rubs her hands like a small child. "Roland will be here in a few minutes. He's taking me out to Grimmwich, and I hope to be an enjoyable companion."

My chin smacks my chest. "The Huntsman is taking you on a date?"

"Yep." She rises to clear the table with a happy little tap dance in her fluffy slippers and then lifts an enquiring brow as she reaches for the plate with Jack's piece of cake on it. I shake my head, so she takes it away with the rest to the sink. "You see, since you kids stopped playing, we found it a bit sad that we don't see each other so often anymore." Turning around with the dishcloth in her hand, she whispers through a grin, "He grew on me."

"With his big knife, slicing Jack open every so often?" I squeak as I take my cup to the sink. "Not on me." And to be frank, I don't really want to be around when the burly man with beard comes and starts courting my Granny. This is so odd.

"Aw, you just don't know him well." She follows me to the door, resting her palm on the small of my back. "You need to start giving people a chance outside of their stories, dear. Get to know them."

"Yeah, right." I did that, and all I got was the bad end of a charade. "I'm fine with the few good friends I have. No need for more."

Lovingly, she strokes my hair and smiles at me. "You'll come to appreciate them when you get older."

"Not getting older in this place," I deadpan and shrug. "Not happening."

Her hand slides down my shoulder and arm when, suddenly, her gaze snags on my cloak and she lifts the ripped corner in front of my nose. "What happened to this?"

Ugh. "I had to tear a strip off to bandage Jack's arm. He did tell you about the fight with the thieves, right?"

"Oh…yes." Her brows arch up in realization as she drops the ragged end of my cape and opens the door for me. Then her face softens with a look that strangely warms me from the inside. "At least now I know what that red band was on Jack's wrist today."

Thunderstruck, I stop on the threshold and whirl around to Granny, but she only grins at my face and closes the door.

Chapter 14

Jack

"Hey, Tweedle—" Aah, what the hell, who cares if it's Dum or Dee. I raise my empty glass, index finger lifted, and murmur with my face pillowed on the bar, "Bring me another scotch. Double." Oh shit, should I have lifted two fingers for that?

If there's one good thing in the smoke-filled *Shady Wonders*, it's the superfast service. A new glass of fine amber liquid appears before me. It's just the right stuff to help me get over the cold look I saw earlier in Riley's eyes. When I lower my swaying arm and reach for the new drink, someone steals it from right in front of my nose. Seconds later, the empty glass slams back on the counter.

"Heeey…" The counter's wooden surface rubs against my cheek, slurring my protest.

A hand claps on my shoulder. "Didn't anybody ever tell you that alcohol isn't a solution?"

"Is that the reason you trash yourself so often?" I counter Eric's rebuke, battling to straighten up so I can send him a mean glare over my shoulder. It would be easier if he stopped splitting into two Erics and then folding back into one.

He and Phillip take the stools on either side and flank me. Phil orders a glass of white wine and a mineral water. I guess Eric had enough with downing my single malt.

"Who's the anti-drink for?" I snarl, flirting with the bar again. With just one more scotch and this lovely, rough pillow, I might finally find the sleep that eluded me all of last night.

Phillip pushes the nasty water in front of me. "You, my friend."

"No, thanks." In my current state, it'll just give me gut cooties.

"You better drink this and then tell us what happened in the Snow Plains because I had a not so pleasant visit from Riley today."

Oh, little Miss Red Riding Hood squealed on me, did she? Didn't take her long. I snatch the water, raise my glass, and toast to the other four. "I screwed up."

"Then fix it." Eric pinches a pretzel stick from the bowl on the counter and shreds it down. "We didn't help you through a prince pimp so you can wimp out now. Royal rule number one: *never give up, no matter what a tough nut your girl is.*"

"And how am I supposed to repair things if she hates me, smartass? You know it's not like she just lost her voice and I'm too stupid to recognize her by anything else."

"Ouch." Eric pouts, half of the pretzel stick squeezed between his lips. "The *smartass* hurt."

"No, seriously." Sighing, I put the glass down and drop my forehead to my folded arms. "This time, I ruined everything with her. I don't see how she'll forgive me for the charade and not telling her for so long."

"Which was, in fact, the dumbest thing you could have done, pal," Phillip says. "Why didn't you tell her somewhere along the way?"

I tilt my head, scrutinizing him and his twin for a couple of seconds. "Excuse me, when did you tell Rory about the broken ice sculpture again? I forgot."

He laughs. "Bite me, son of a Wolf."

I flip him off and lower my head again, but something tugs at the band around my right wrist. "What's this? Did you hurt yourself?" Eric demands.

"No. It's a piece from Riley's cloak."

"And you wear it like a bracelet, why?"

"Because she gave it to me." And I can't bring myself to toss it away. "If there's nothing left of her in my life, then at least I have this token."

"Ah," Phil groans next to me. "Perhaps you should give her something of yours to wear, too. To make her understand you mean it."

"Right. Like what?" I growl in frustration. "My leather jacket?" Hah. She'd be so happy to wear it. I roll my eyes in the hollow of my arms.

"No," he answers flatly. "But maybe a ring."

Slowly, I lift my head.

Phillip stares at me, dead serious. And then he arches an eyebrow.

*

It's much too silent in my apartment. The sounds from Honeypot Square beneath my window died shortly after sunset. A long shower and finally a few hours of sleep helped to clear away the haze from my mind. But now I'm lying in bed with my arms folded behind my head, studying the ceiling in the dark, and nothing has changed from this morning. The wrenching feeling in my chest is still killing me.

Shit, I miss her. Will the pain ever go away? I know it's only been a day now, and my friends promised me it would get better after a while but, frankly, I just can't imagine that.

I wish we could play again—Little Red Riding Hood and the Wolf, or any other damn story out there. I wouldn't even mind if I got skewered ten times in the same tale as long as she was in it.

In the Winter Suite at Minvendeen's Edge, Riley said she didn't feel the tug of our story anymore. And I know that even without Dr. Jekyll's elixir, I wouldn't either. Because our tale is broken. She was right yesterday—it wasn't *her* ever after that cracked the night of the ball. It was *mine*. And if I learned one thing from her on this adventure, it's that only a kiss of true love can do that.

So why in the world does she doubt my intentions? Why does she refuse to believe that I'm truly in love with her and that it wasn't just a stupid game?

But, of course, I know the answer. She's wounded. In her quest to find the perfect ever after, she was extremely vulnerable—she opened up to me about her secret desires, after all. And I, like an idiot, hurt her. Without meaning to. If only she gave me a chance to explain everything.

If only she knew my story from the beginning to the very end.

But what is the *very end* anyway? I swallow. Whatever I can tell her, it would still be unfinished, for she alone holds my end in her hands. Rolling my head to the side, I gaze through the window at the bright moon in the star-filled sky. He's cried so many tears over happy endings...and none of them were for me.

Does he cry for me now when he looks down and sees my pain and struggle? Probably not, because anything that happened between Riley and me was beyond all official tales. If it's not in a storybook, it never happened.

All of a sudden, my breath catches in my lungs. With a flash of adrenaline jolting through my body, I brace myself up on my elbows and stare harder at the moon. "Is that it?"

Of course, the damn, fat orb is silent, but the twinkle of the second star to the right fills me with hope, warming my cold insides. What if this is my chance to explain myself to Riley, even if she doesn't want to listen?

I switch on the lamp on my nightstand and go on a raid through the drawers until I find an old, leather-bound notepad and a pen. The thing is covered in ancient dust, which I blow off and then settle back against the headboard. With my knees bent and the book supported against them, I open it to the first page. Gripped by an entirely new excitement, I begin to write.

My Ever After…

Chapter 15

Riley

Over the last couple of days, I read and reread *Harry Potter and the Prisoner of Azkaban*, knowing quite well by doing so, I made the poor wizard go through hell twice in a row. At least his story has a good ending, the guy can't complain. But a third time would be torture.

So when the sun starts to descend in the west, I slip on my boots, grab the book, and head off to Grimmwich to return it to the library. Perhaps I can pick up a new adventure tale from there to keep me distracted during the night.

Reading stories is so much different than playing them. It's nice entertainment, except all the real feelings are missing. I couldn't quite connect with the terrifying pull of the dementors, couldn't hear the cry of the hippogriff, and couldn't see the light exploding from Harry's wand when he called upon his patronus.

When I used to walk through the Wood of 1000 Dawns as Red Riding Hood, the magic there was tangible at all times. The moss and the trees wove their alluring scent around me, the ripple of the Timeless Brook soothed my mind, and bee stings actually hurt. Overcome by a sudden wave of melancholy, I clutch the book harder to my chest. Jack's first smile always warmed a small spot inside my heart…

As I reach Grimmwich in the evening glow, the last sunrays of the day gleam off the tall windows of Gulliver's Travelshop, drawing my attention. I stop and stare at my reflection. The sad face hiding inside a red hood looks so very unfamiliar. Although she has the same eyes, nose, and mouth as I do, the girl is a stranger. Is this what people look like when they lose their tales? Or do they maybe look like this after they've lost their love? A sigh escapes me, and I sniff...

Then I remember what happened.

Argh! How can I still miss that nasty piece of work after everything he did to me?

Grinding my teeth in frustration, I stride down Bookpage Avenue to the library at the corner and push open the doors. A gentle wind brushes across my face at my entry, and the whisper of a thousand tales slithers along my skin. A wilted smell clings to the three-story place with its shelves divided into sections named after the parts of Fairyland and outside where all the stories happen.

Only a handful of people have come here this late, leisurely strolling through the rows of shelves to find their next story fix. Pushing my hood down, I head straight to Hogwarts and put Harry back into the empty slot. Unfortunately, his sequel adventure is missing. Belle must still have it under her pillow. She was the one who infected me with curiosity about the boy in the first place. Since I don't want to skip a part of the saga, I head back to the exit empty-handed today. The faster I'm out again, the better it is because the constant buzzing in the library always gives me a headache after a while. When I pass the shelf of the Wood of 1000 Dawns, however, my steps falter.

My eyes swipe across the titles vertically lined up. There are Princess Belle's and Cindy's books, the *Frog Prince*, and the *Golden Goose*. Someone put *Hansel and Gretel* upside down in its place, so I take it out and flip it right. And then my gaze snags on an unimposing dark red book next to it with golden letters in the title.

Little Red Riding Hood.

With a shaky hand, I reach for it. It's funny that I've never thought to take out my own story before. There was no need to because I knew every single line of the journey by heart. As I slowly slide the book out of its place, the whisper of a wolf howl brushes my neck, and the merry tune of a girl quietly drifts from faraway to me. Shivers run through me, making me squeeze my eyes tight for a single moment. When I cast a timid look around, I find people engrossed in their own reading, sitting in wingback chairs or standing in front of the shelves. No one but me seems to hear what I do. Maybe because this is *my* story and not theirs.

But if I hear it, Granny might, too. And Jack…

Now that our tale is broken, I wonder how long it will be until we start to forget. What happens if we never play again? Will I remember that I used to pack red wine and marble cake, Granny's favorite, at the beginning? And a hundred years from now, will I still know that Jack always wore a band t-shirt of the Town Musicians of Bremen under his black leather jacket at our first meeting?

Will I still be wearing my red cloak then?

Looking down, I stroke the velvety fabric, gently kneading the ripped corner. Just what shall I do with the rest of my life without my place in a tale? The thought sends unpleasant goosebumps over my skin. It sounds like an eternity of wandering blindly, of being homeless and alone.

Dang it, Jack is an idiot. But before last weekend, at least he was *my* idiot. Our story was nothing special, short and unspectacular. Yet today, it seems like it's always been the world to me. How could I have been so stupid to kick myself out of it? From the empty feeling inside me, there's no going back.

Or is there?

I bite the inside of my cheek, shifting my mouth to one side. What will happen if…? My narrow-eyed look drops to the fine red book in my hands. Technically, it should be possible. I open the first page that holds a picture of a girl in a neat dress and a cloak, carrying a small basket through the forest. This is where it all began.

The tiny hairs on the back of my neck bristle as I inhale deeply. Then I clear my throat and read out loud:

"Once upon a time, there was a dear little girl who was loved by everyone who looked at her—"

"Shhh!" the harsh warning carries from several directions at once.

A gasp escapes me and, in a panic, I jump backward, snapping the book shut. The thud echoes from the shelves. My embarrassed gaze flies around the room, meeting censorious faces everywhere.

For Grimm's sake, what was I thinking? Am I really so desperate to get my job back that I'd condone Jack's appalling deceit? Not playing must have gotten to my head. Or maybe the indistinct whispering of the many stories in this old building did.

A longing to escape from this place takes hold of me. I press my own story to my chest and make a wild dash for the exit.

"Miss?" the old librarian with horn-rimmed, fishbowl glasses sitting low on her nose shouts after me. "You need to register the book if you want to take it out!"

Whirling around, I stumble backward. "I—I'll bring it back tomorrow!" I answer her and fall through the door, out of this mystical place. The air whizzes from my lungs as I rumble down the stairs and finally come to lie still on my back. *Whoa.*

Trying to catch my breath again, my gaze fastens on the golden letters arching like a rainbow above the door. *Grimmwich Library. You play it, we stock it.*

Slowly sitting up on the sidewalk in front of the stairs, I look down at the red leather-bound book in my lap. The whispering howl and the brushing melody have stopped, just like the purring over my skin from the other tales inside. My fingertips trace the embossed words on the cover. It's simple, yet so beautiful—like the forest, like my cottage, like my cloak. A strange feeling comes over me as if everything I ever called home is packed inside this little book. Would somebody miss *Little Red Riding Hood* in the library if I didn't return it at all?

I draw in a deep breath and then slip the book into the inside pocket of my cloak. Since no one plays this story any longer, it's only fair that they don't have it in stock.

"Watch out!" A shrill cry behind me makes me jump. I whip around and find myself face-to-face with a Dalmatian avalanche. In wild terror, I throw my arms over my head and curl up in a ball on the sidewalk, feeling a gazillion whelps leaping over my body and scampering around me.

"So sorry!" Cruella screeches as she, too, teeters past in

her stiletto high-heels, from the sound of it, racing after the furry pack she's apparently sitting today.

Even after the storm is over, I don't dare move on the ground but only pry one eyelid open. A hairy muzzle waits inches from my nose, the rest of the attached meatball rocking hard from its wiggling tail.

Quickly, I straighten and make room for him to pass, but the little fella doesn't even think to run after his friends. Instead, he skids toward me, sitting back down every few inches and excitedly wagging his tail. I watch him sideways with narrowed eyes. Heck, he's one of the cutest little things I've seen in a long time. His tongue hangs out from a mouth that looks as if a baby smile is pasted on it, and his black ears rise and fall with every little bit he moves forward.

Something about his huge, dark eyes reminds me of Jack when he's in wolf form. They don't let me out of sight for even one second, so I lift my little buddy into my arms. He's cozy and cuddly, his small front paws on my shoulder trying to catch a hold. "What do you want from me, puppy dog?" I croak. "You should hurry on and catch up with your hundred siblings."

When the cute furball licks my face, my throat tightens.

"Jasper!" The brisk clacking of high-heels on the concrete returns. "Oh, there you are."

Climbing to my feet, I hand the spotted bundle over to Cruella, who gives me a quick red-lipped smile framed by curtains of black and white hair. She puts him under her arm, backside forward, where he blends in with her fancy dotted fur coat. As she races off again after the hoard of doggie toddlers, Jasper's head wobbles up and down, his tongue still lolling out in the sweetest little puppy smile. Feebly, I wave at him until his taxi rounds the corner, then my hand sinks to my chest. A spot inside there stings quite badly.

A couple of minutes pass, but neither Jasper nor the pack of hounds returns. Eventually, I heave a deep sigh and head home.

All the way out of Grimmwich and through the forest, the encounter with the puppy dog has me thinking. Why have I never gotten a pet? A dog or even a cat in the cabin would make the place a lot cozier for sure. So what kept me from taking a fury orphan home?

As I near the signpost in the woods, the answer strikes me—as simple as it is obvious. Jack. I did have a pet of sorts all this time, didn't I? Even if the big, bad Wolf wasn't quite so cuddly over the years. That only changed last week when we started spending real time together. And I liked hanging out with him.

What might have become of us if we did this earlier, when we still had our tale? Absently, my fingers brush my lips. Would we have kissed at some point anyway? A small smile tugs at my lips. Possibly…

Jiminy Cricket! I tear my gaze away from the signpost because only now I realize how hard I was staring at it. And for how long. Shaking my head to loosen the harebrained thought, I stride along the path and head home to Glitter Hollow.

Once back in my cottage, I close the windows, take off my boots and coat, and put a pot of milk on the stove to make a cup of hot chocolate. With all the furry thinking, it doesn't appear that I'll be sleeping any better tonight than I did yesterday, so slurping a sweet drink to keep me warm through the dark hours sounds like a better plan.

As the milk slowly heats, I sink onto the sofa and take a quick look into *Little Red Riding Hood*. Reading the first line at the library earlier did nothing to restart the pull of the story inside me. It was stupid to even try. After all, I don't want to play alongside a liar for the rest of my life. Better not to play at all.

Or is it?

My face scrunches. By the thirteen fairies, I don't know…

The pictures continuing throughout the book as I thumb through the pages capture my attention. I read a few lines of page eleven, where the girl and the Wolf have a conversation beneath the trees. A laugh escapes me. Oh dear, do we really sound this silly when we play? I don't think so. Our story must have twisted away from the original in several places over time. Especially since, in this book, Jack also eats me before the end.

I settle deeper into the cushions of the couch and pull my feet up onto the sofa, flipping back to the very first page. Let's see what Grimm really had in mind for us when he scribbled down my story with his brother.

My feet stuffed beneath a blanket, I giggle my way through the book. In some of Jack's dialogue, he sounds like he's got stones in his mouth. Such a funny language—one would need a dictionary for certain words.

At every turn of another page, the musty scent of the paper fans into my face. It smells like it's ten thousand years old. After some minutes, a nasty whiff adds to the odor. Reminds me of burnt toast. Holy gingerbread house, what have they done to the book? Baked it in the Mean Witch's oven? I finish the page, but the stench is getting really intense, and my vision seems a bit foggy, too. This can't possibly be from the book.

Quirking my eyebrows, I look up and scan around. A light mist looms in the cottage, carrying an acrid smell. *Ugh.* With a thud, I snap *Little Red Riding Hood* shut and jump up from the sofa. Where the heck is the smell coming from?

In the next instant, a loud sizzle from the stove makes me jerk around. Oh, dang—the milk!

Panic flooding me, I dash to the fireplace where a foamy white mass slops over the edge of the pot and dribbles onto the glow. More fumes rise from the burnt milk inside the pot. The stinking smoke fills my entire house and my lungs, causing me to cough violently. One corner of my cloak functioning as a potholder and the other pushed over my mouth and nose, I pull the pot from the fire and bolt across the room and out through the door. The smolder might draw some Indians to my house, I don't care. Better them than smoking myself out.

In utter darkness, I trip over a loose board on the porch and plunge forward. The pot flies out of my hand, tumbling down the stairs while I brake hard with my forehead against the column that holds up the roof.

Ouch!

I crumple to the floor where I take a couple of seconds laying sprawled on my back, my head touching the stair below. Are the stars in front of my eyes real?

When some disappear while others stay in the sky above the porch roof, I suppose the worst is over—except for a pounding headache.

Moaning, I rub my brow and battle into a seated position. My house dances around me. Stupid floorboard. I need to get that fixed, and fast. With some help from the pole, I drag myself up and decide to leave the burnt pot in the grass where it can smoke out until the morning. It'll take hours to scrub it clean anyway.

My body aching from my fall, I head back for the door, but something small on the porch, illuminated by the light falling out from the living room, catches my eye. What is this, another book? I pick it up and find that there's a note tied to the brown leather cover. I must have tripped over it in my dash outside. Turns out, the board isn't loose, after all.

My eyes narrow as I spin around and scan the dark.

Delivery weasels don't usually work so late. Besides, they would have knocked on the door. So who brought this? Since it's night and I can't see a thing, I head back inside and close the door. Grimacing at the ache in my forehead, I lower onto the couch, the book on my lap.

With an impatient tug on the cord, the tie loosens. The note, a folded piece of paper, falls off. Curious, I open it and instantly recognize the brawny handwriting. My heart pounds faster, and I cut a look at the door. Did Jack drop the book on my porch?

My gaze back on the note, I read the two lines standing out against the white.

They say stories need to be written down to really happen.
Grimm was a bastard because he didn't write my ending with you.

The sadness in those few words descends on me in a strange way, as if they connect right with the splinter of my heart that still misses Jack. My throat tightens, and the note slips from my weak fingers. Breathing harder, I slowly open the book.

My Ever After
An unfinished tale by Jack Wolf

In silent shock, I clap one hand over my mouth as I let the pages run through my fingers and find they are filled with a thousand lines in Jack's hand. It must have taken him days to write all of this. My goodness…

But why? Is this another version of our story? *Little Red Riding Hood and the Wolf?*

With no idea what to expect, I pull my legs up and rest the book on my forearms. Clasping the top edges, I begin to read.

Once upon a time, there was the loveliest young girl, and with everything she did and said, she dug her way deeper into my heart. Unfortunately, it took me an eternity to figure that out, and I probably never would have, if she hadn't decided to kick me out of her ending one day. The girl's name was Riley Redcoat, but you may have heard her called Little Red Riding Hood…

A tiny, wondrous smile tugs at my mouth at the sweet opening.

In Fairyland, we play stories every day. Riley and I have acted out ours so often, I can recite every line in my sleep. That one morning where my tale actually began, I had to do just that…play with only one eye open because we were summoned to the Wood of 1000 Dawns in the dead of night. This is rare, and I totally needed a drink afterward. The Shady Wonders is a fine address for that. I like the music in the pub. It's the reason I go there so often. For the band, the scotch, and to play pool with Phil and Eric...

The way he describes the morning at the *Shady Wonders* and his friendship with the two princes warms my heart. Reading on about what he felt throughout the day I decided to run from our tale and find something else does so even more. The fact that I thought King Arthur could give me that *something* feels utterly stupid now.

> *Riley was an excellent archer. She could shoot a cherry off a tree from three hundred feet away. Six feet of king flesh a short distance from us wasn't much of a challenge. If I'd let her fire the arrow, I would have lost her without a doubt. I would have lost our tale and my job, too. She would have turned my whole life upside down with just one shot.*
> *Panic rose inside me, hot like the coals in her granny's stove. I couldn't let her do this. Not so fast. Not today!*

My gaze hardens because this is proof that I was right. Jack *was* scared to lose our tale. His job. It had nothing to do with love as he tried to make me believe.

But as the pages fly by and I come to the part where he locked himself in Phillip's dungeon to protect me from the big, bad Wolf, my chest suddenly constricts. The pain, the desperation, and the confusion he felt when he couldn't free himself of the Wolf anymore tears at my heartstrings. Pictures of the night on the cold dungeon floor press into my mind when I stroked Jack's head for hours, praying he would be all right.

I turn page after page, devouring every word as he drags me ever deeper into his—*our*—tale. The book gives me glimpses into his mind that make me laugh out loud at times when he writes about my kiss challenge with the frogs or the fun we had in the haystack. Minutes later, a mist shrouds my vision as he reveals what he really felt that night in my house when we sat in front of the fire together. How he wanted to touch me, play with my hair, and tried to think up a way to become my prince.

I can only imagine what kind of crap Phillip and Eric made him go through the next morning to change him into Jacob. Never underestimate three guys with a solid but entirely silly plan.

Learning about the time after the ball, when Jack thought he'd killed me with a kiss, is my undoing. I break out in sobs, dabbing quickly at the tears trailing down my cheeks so I can read on about our journey to the Snow Plains.

The realization of why he was so quiet in the mountains, why he couldn't actually bring himself to throw the strip of my cloak away, fills me with a longing to find Jack tonight and just hold him. To hug him tightly for everything he took on his shoulders to make me happy.

And when we came home, I knew I couldn't keep the truth from her any longer. She needed to know who

I don't know what to say. In fact, I don't even know how to breathe anymore after this because I'm sobbing so hard. It feels like the day I left him behind and ran home, shutting him out of my life, only happened minutes ago. Remorse strikes me hard, I'm unspeakably sorry. Aching. And alone.

I close my eyes, fighting to keep all the pain inside and stop the burning tears from falling. It's impossible. I never wanted to hurt Jack like this, but all I ever saw were the things my friends had—the ever after I longed for and couldn't have with a Wolf in my story. And then, when I found out about his betrayal, it stung too much for me to stay. I couldn't...after falling in love with him.

Sniffing, I wipe the tears away from my eyes and read the final lines on the last page.

I don't know if my heart wants to melt or explode inside my chest at his last words. The only thing I can say for sure is that it wants out into the Wood of 1000 Dawns to find Jack at our spot. Lowering the book, I look up and notice with surprise that I've been reading through the entire night. Morning is breaking outside the windows.

Suddenly, an urgent thought grips me. Will he be there? Right now?

There's only one way to find out. I don't want to waste another minute.

Pulling on my boots, I drape the red cloak around my shoulders and pick up the book from the sofa before sprinting outside. On the porch, I close my eyes and inhale deeply. The crisp morning air fills my burning chest, the familiar smell of the woods and the early morning chirping of the birds in the trees soothing my tension. They give me hope that I'm heading off into my happy ending.

With every step I take along the path, the wings of my heart grow bigger. My pulse is banging against the base of my throat like an excited chicken.

Just a few more steps…the last bend to go around. There's only one spot in this world that Jack would call *ours*. The signpost. And if he isn't standing beneath it yet, then I'll wait all day for him to find me there.

A single, warm sunray breaks through the leaves and

tickles my nose. As I tilt my head up, a round of robins rises, forming a perfect circle in the soft pink morning sky. My skin begins to prickle. Feeling a hopeful smile lifting the corners of my mouth, I hug the book tighter to my chest and round the bend. And then, all stories in the world pause for a timeless moment when I see him.

Jack sits on the ground, his back against the signpost, his legs bent, and his arms loosely braced on his knees. The sleeves of his black sweatshirt are pushed up to his elbows, and the red strip of my cloak it tied around his right wrist. My steps falter as our eyes meet. Wonder, hope, and fear loom in his. Who knows how long he's been waiting there for me? But from the intense and longing look he sends my way, it may have been forever.

Both of us are rooted to the spot. We just stare at each other from ten feet apart. Jack is as gorgeous as ever, only the dark rings under his eyes give proof that he hasn't slept much lately.

What does he expect from me now? Honestly, I don't know. He poured his entire soul into the book I'm pressing to my chest, and I want nothing more than to run to him and fling my arms around his neck. But fear holds me back because he doesn't move either.

I take a timid step forward then stop again. "Jack…?" My voice breaks, and he just blinks. If only he would tell me to come to him. I'd run. I swear I'd hug him and give him my heart. But his silence freezes me. "I don't know what to say."

He holds my gaze captive for another long moment, then he slowly rises, pats the dirt from his jeans, and pushes his hands into the pockets. My breathing hitches as he walks toward me.

His focus never sways from me, not for a single step. When he finally stands right in front of me, and I have to lift my chin to look into his face, he shoves his fingers into my hair, stroking his thumb across my cheek. "I miss you."

There it is…so simple…yet saying so much. I swallow, my throat painfully tight. "I miss you, too."

Jack opens his mouth to say something else, but then he breaks off and, with gentle fingers, brushes my bangs away from the sore bump on my forehead, his brows furrowing. "Did you try to turn into a unicorn?"

Ashamed of the date with the pole last night, I lower my head. "Something like that…"

Both his hands shape to my cheeks now, and he lifts my face to make me look into his beautiful, dark eyes. A tiny diamond sparkles in each of them. "Since you came," he whispers, "can I make a wish?"

"*Any*—" There's no sound at all coming from my mouth, only my lips move, so I nod.

He blinks, tilting his head slightly to one side. A hopeful gleam enters his look. "If you don't mind…I would like to keep you forever."

My eyes fill with tears, but I hold them back. Instead, I smile at Jack with all the love I feel for him. "Forever is a long time in Fairyland."

His gaze drops to my mouth. As I half close my eyes, he leans in until his lips come to lie against mine and breathes, "Not nearly long enough, honeydrop." And then we kiss upon a star.

He lets me get a taste of him with only a soft touch to my upper lip. Once, twice. His tantalizing scent fills my head until I believe I'm lying in a field of snowdrops. When he opens my mouth with a hungry little growl, the forest around us comes to life with the first tender touch of our tongues.

Inching back from him, I open my eyes and look around in wonder. Squirrels peek at us from branches. Foxes and bunnies sit like friends next to each other in the bushes, peering at us, and a round of robins draws their circle above our heads. "We've got witnesses," I whisper in stunned surprise.

Jack's hands are still on my cheeks, and he gazes at me roguishly as he brings my lips right back to his. "Don't we always?" The next instant, he takes my mouth with a fierceness only the ending of a story can bring. Our tongues dance, our lips mingle. It barely gives me a moment to breathe. And I love it…because I love *him*.

The book holding all the truth of his feelings for me slips from my arms and drops to the ground between us. As I lay my palms against his chest, warm ripples of happiness trail through my body because his heart is beating so strongly, telling me that I've finally found my place in the story. Jack was right, forever is just the perfect time to spend with him. I never should have doubted it.

After our lips meet once more for the last tender kiss to seal our wish, he rests his forehead against mine, sighing deeply.

"And now?" I send him a tentative smile. "Will we be living happily ever after?"

A chuckle rocks his chest as he wraps his arms around me and snuggles me close. "I guess not." With his chin placed on top of my head, he teases, "We'll probably argue a lot, and I might snap at your ass from time to time." He pauses, and the chuckle fades. "But in the end, it doesn't matter..." He presses a soft kiss to my brow. "Because, honestly, I can't think of a more beautiful ending to our story than this."

I close my eyes as I agree.

Chapter 16

Jack

It's been days since Riley found her way to me in the Wood of 1000 Dawns and we sealed the crack in our tale. After everything we botched up, I almost didn't dare believe the call of *Little Red Riding Hood* would set in again. But it did. And playing our story with Riley this morning felt like the very first time.

It was perfect.

"Granny was so mad that she got eaten again, did you notice?" Riley asks me on the way home to her cottage.

Our fingers laced, I draw her closer and smirk down at

her. "She was just pissed because we burst in on her date with the Huntsman. In truth, she loves the excitement we bring into her life every time we play."

"You might be right." She clings to my arm with her other hand and rests her head on my shoulder. I love the dreamy sigh that always escapes her when she's utterly happy.

We've had the best time this past week. Two months ago, I wouldn't have believed for a minute that sharing a tale and my life with the honeydrop was all I would ever need to feel at home. And I bet she hadn't either.

There's only one little thing missing to make it complete. I've been toying with the thought for a while, but before I bring it up, I had to have the dwarfs make something for me. Dopey brought it to my apartment this morning, and I was on my way to Riley when the familiar call of the story set in, putting my plans on hold.

But now, I don't want to wait any longer.

As we reach her homey little cottage in the evening glow, Riley offers to make us hot chocolate. I stop near the pole of the porch rail. "Not now."

She turns around, scrutinizing me sideways. "You don't want to come in?"

I shrug and lean against the post. "Maybe later. I like sunsets on your veranda." The left side of my mouth twitches up. "Reminds me of interesting times I spent here."

"Okay, let's stay out here then." Grinning, she lowers

to the top step of the porch. When I don't move away from the railing, she points to the west. "Jack, the sunset is that way."

"I know." My eyes remain fastened on her.

"You're looking in the wrong direction if you want to see it."

"I don't think so."

Her face scrunches, so I tell her, "I like to watch the glow of the last rays reflect in your eyes." They always sparkle like golden honey. I don't think I'll ever get enough of this view.

Riley shakes her head. "You're crazy, puppy dog."

"Yeah, maybe I am." With a smirk, I push away from the railing, lower myself behind her, my legs spread so she sits between them, and press a quick kiss to her neck. "Only over you."

A snicker escapes her, and I love it.

My arms wrapped around her stomach, I pull her against my chest, and together we watch the sun melting into the treetops. The warm glow fills me with confidence and happiness because I have everything I need right here with me.

"Have I told you that I love you?" I whisper in her ear.

Riley tilts her head to the side, gazing blissfully into my eyes. "I figured that out from a line or two in the book you wrote me."

I wrinkle my nose. "The book is a bit cumbersome to always carry around and remind you of it, don't you think?"

"That's why I keep it on my nightstand," she teases.

"Want something smaller to remind you instead?" I fetch something from my pocket and then take her hand. "Maybe to wear on your finger?"

"What?" With a confused laugh, Riley looks down and watches as I slip the golden band with the amber drop set into the middle on her ring finger. Her giggles fade, and her eyes widen. "Jack, what...?" she croaks in a hoarse voice.

"Let's be Red Riding Hood and the Wolf forever." Tenderly, I intertwine our fingers, waiting for her to look at me. When she does, and her mouth is still open, I close it with a small kiss. "Please, be mine."

Staring at me as if my last change into the Wolf went wrong and I became Olaf the Snowman, she lets me wait fifteen fucking seconds for her answer. I count every single one with a drumming heart.

Until, eventually, her face splits with a wide smile that makes her honey eyes shine like little stars in the night sky.

And she nods.

Riley

Jack and I had to play really early this morning, which left me a little grumpy. Heck, I'm just not a morning person. And it's Sunday, too, which makes me late to the meeting with the girls in Princess Cinderella's castle. I love this tradition. Cindy always has macarons. They are soo yummy. The red ones are the best.

I slip through the heavy door, cringing at the loud thud when it falls closed. Laughter from the parlor upstairs drifts to me. Obviously, the tea party is in full swing, so I quickly toe off my boots and hang the bow and quiver on a hook. Then I dash upstairs and run down the corridor.

Princess Snow-White, Aurora, Belle, and Cindy are seated around the neat, white coffee table, sipping tea from delicate china cups. Once again, they are all dressed in marvelous, colorful gowns, which I still envy at times. But not so much anymore since I know that Jack loves me best in my red cloak. Granny made me a brand new one last week. She said it's improper for a sweet girl to walk around with a ripped one.

I wave at my friends and then slump down next to Snow-White on the noble sofa with its gold-embroidered blue cushions. Her skirt accidentally gets trapped beneath me. As she tries to tug it free, a quick flash of déjà vu grips me. Quirking my eyebrows, I lift my bottom to set the skirt free.

Cindy slides a cup of strawberry tea across the table in front of me. "Hey, why the suspicious look, sweetie?" Her porcelain face splits with a grin as she leans forward, briefly blocking the beams of sunlight floating into the warm room through the five tall windows. "Plotting something again?"

"Huh? *Ugh.*" I draw my eyebrows even deeper, rubbing my butt cheek that holds a nice set of fang marks from Jack this morning. "No…"

Belle snickers into her teacup and nods toward my hand on the aching spot. "I bet the Wolf bit her again."

"Yeah, he did," I grumble, confirming the rumor. "Do you girls even know how lucky you are? I bet your princes don't snap in your stories like my Wolf does!" I pick up the chipped cup on its saucer. "I want me a prince, too!"

A collective gasp sounds out as every princess in the room freezes. Me, too.

Rory sits up straighter and lowers her chin, skeptically narrowing her eyes at me. "What did you just say?"

The shock of realization shoots through me, stopping my heart. Only my eyes move from her to Belle and Snow-White, ending on Cindy's face. She stares at me with wide, sparkling blue gems, her mouth hanging open, just like mine. Then, a few moments later, the corners twitch up into an impish grin. Slowly, she reaches for the platter on the table, holds it out to me, and arches her eyebrows as she tips her head to the side. "Macaron?"

Holy once upon a time! "I gotta go!" The next instant, I jump from the couch and make a wild dash for the door, gripping the frame to catapult myself around the corner.

"See you at the market tomorrow!" Rory calls after me, laughing out loud with the others. "And don't forget to bring Cupid's arrow!"

A grin tugs hard at my mouth as I race down the marble stairs, slip on my boots, fetch my bow and quiver from the hook, and leave Castle Grove. I need to see Jack!

Not bothering to run home first, I crisscross through the Wood of 1000 Dawns because I know exactly where to find him. Right before the last bend to the crossroads, my steps finally slow. A new wave of nervousness surges up within me. Lifting my hand to my mouth, I bite my thumbnail.

Did he feel it, too? Has he come?

At a brief glance at the sky, my heart swells to twice its size. The robins are flying.

Breathing much too fast, I follow the path around the corner. And then a tank of excitement explodes inside me as I see Jack leaning against the signpost, hands tucked in the pockets of his leather jacket, one leg angled, and his foot flat against the pole. His dark eyes glint through the wild, multihued strands of black and brown falling over his forehead as he watches me draw nearer.

With my head angled, I come to a halt in front of him and ask with a probing edge to my voice, "You went to the pub after we played this morning, didn't you?"

Without a word, Jack slips one arm around me and pulls me flush against him for a hard kiss. The taste of scotch still clings to his tongue, and he lets me lick it off.

"But how is this possible?" I whisper as I lean back moments later.

"Told you." He winks at me. "Stories need to be written down to really happen."

I confront him with a snide look. "But someone also needs to read them, and the true tale of you and me is still on my nightstand."

"Mmh…" Nonchalantly, he drapes an arm around my shoulders and lifts his chin as he walks me away from the signpost, anywhere but the direction of Granny's house. Mischief sparkles in his eyes as he gazes down at me sideways. "Could be that I placed a copy of it at the Grimmwich Library after you said *yes*."

My eyebrows shoot up. "You wouldn't!"

"No? Then tell me, honeydrop, would you rather turn around now and visit your grandmother?"

No freaking way! Even if I wanted to, I couldn't because the call of a different story is so strong it fills up my entire being. My beam getting ever brighter, I shake my head.

Jack grins right back, pulling me along. "I didn't think so."

As the rippling of the Timeless Brook drifts to us, and the little wooden bridge to the Plush Toy Forest appears ahead, a sudden thought hits me right upside the head, and I freeze. His arm slips from my shoulders. "Is everything all right?"

Feeling how my knees get weak, I can only shake my head when I face him and clap my hands over my mouth. "I'm so sorry, Jack."

His forehead creases in lines of confusion. "What for?"

"That you have to go through all the trouble again. The night in Phillip's dungeons, the worry when I disappeared from the ball." My chest constricts. "And then the days after you told me the truth…"

A tender smile appears on his lips, wiping away all the worry from his look. "I'm not sorry at all."

"You're not?"

"No." He cups my face and presses a gentle kiss to my

mouth. "Because at every ending…I get you."

A confident warmth envelops me. He's right. Every little stone on the way was absolutely worth what we have now. All the laughter, all the pain. All the insecurity and all our magical moments. I wouldn't want to miss even one minute of our tale, just like I wouldn't trade my lover for any royal in Fairyland.

And from the intense look he gives me, Jack wouldn't either.

He laces our fingers, and together, we face the bridge across the Timeless Brook. "Ready?" he asks me with a wolfish smirk.

I squeeze his hand and smile right back.

And they lived happily

ever after...

I hope it's okay to add a few words for you here. Personal words. Things that absorbed me entirely while writing this fairy tale.

It's the truth about the Neverwind…

My entire life I chased a world I felt was out there somewhere. Deep inside me, I knew it was *home*, I just didn't know how to get there. But it's a funny thing with *thinking* you know something and actually *understanding* it.

I would like you to answer one question for yourself. Do you believe in fairy tales?

I don't need to believe in fairy tales and magic because I live in them. It's like when you say you don't need to believe in your own house because you can see the doors, the windows, the walls all around you and the roof above your head.

Boy, it was a long way to get home. The path was steep and rocky. But it also became the most beautiful journey I've ever been on. Piece by piece I came to understand how the rack-wheels of this other world functioned. Because in truth, I was in the room with the magic all along. It just took a while until my eyes opened.

Writing is a very magical and powerful instrument. It's the key to a certain door that leads into the world of a reality that you only know as fairy tales. I'm one of the lucky ones—I found the right door. To me, the Otherworld is more real than anything you can see on this planet.

If you followed me until here and aren't shaking your head right now, maybe you're even on the doorstep to this fantastic world yourself. Did the Neverwind already brush your face and play with your hair? Are you getting goosebumps right now, only thinking about it? Well, perhaps then you're qualified to learn the truth. The truth about fairy tales...

Writing Jack and Riley's story was a magical experience for me, like every other book I wrote so far. And I'm speaking of magic because it's the only word that does this process justice. Everybody born into this world comes with a certain talent. Some may create amazing music that makes people's hearts bleed with emotion, some get flashes of an adventurous future and create awesome technical stuff, and others might be good with kids or people in general. Whatever it is, every single person has a special talent.

My gift is to build bridges from the Otherworld to Earth.

I'm deliberately not using the term "to reality" because for me both worlds are exactly the same kind of real. They only differ in their substance.

The world that you all know is firm and compact. You can touch things and see them with your eyes. The Otherworld is very subtle. Etheric. You touch it with your mind and your heart rather than with your hands. But if you allow yourself to let this other reality be true, you'll be able to wander among that world as if there was no difference. Well, there is… One. The Otherworld is so much bigger and more beautiful than anything you'll ever see on Earth.

For a very long time I used to think stories are floating in a certain sphere which for a lack of name I just called *The Ether*. Jack and Riley recently told me it's actually called the Neverwind.

Think of it like Beings with particular stories are born in a place that may or may not be called the Rhymeshire. From there, the Neverwind picks up their essence and carries it through space and time. So when this special wind brushes a person with a wide-open mind, these people can connect with the characters and hear their stories. But they don't just hear them. They also see them, feel them, and live those lives. Being touched by the Neverwind is an invitation from those creatures to follow them into the Otherworld and make their tale come true by writing it down. It'll manifest with every word on a page.

Believe me when I say the word *Imagination* has been used completely the wrong way since the beginning of time. People use it for things they think aren't real. But the truth is, Imagination is so much more. It can be a tool, an escape, and sometimes even a weapon. Imagination, for me, is the most powerful thing on Earth because it *is* the key & door to this other, really existing world.

Higher mathematics is an absolute riddle to me, something I'll never understand. But I don't doubt for a second that it is real after all.

And it's the same with Imagination, the Otherworld, the Neverwind, the floating stories, and the wonderful creatures. You don't need to understand them. You don't even need to believe in them if you decide you don't want to. It will, in fact, change nothing about their existence. Because they *are* real.

And on every single day of my life, I'm thankful for their invitation into this wonderful world of fairy tales. I don't think I could breathe in *The Reality*, if this door to *home* was closed for me.

ANNA KATMORE
NEVER LAND

DREAMS OF NEVER EVER book 1

Strange things happen in Neverland…

Angelina McFarland has always loved fairy tales — but she never dreamed she'd one day fall right into one. Literally.

Swept from her world into a land of lost boys, fairies, and whispered secrets, Angel is rescued by a mysterious flying boy who refuses to grow up — and captured by a pirate whose smile is every bit as dangerous as his blade.

Desperate to escape the island's curse — and the clutches of a ship called the *Jolly Roger* — she's drawn into a timeless game where loyalty wavers, hearts are stolen, and every wish comes with a price.

But as days turn into stolen nights beneath the stars of Neverland, Angel begins to wonder if the infamous Captain Hook is truly the villain of this story…or the hero she was never meant to forget.

So grab a happy thought and follow Angel on an adventure that will sweep you off your feet — and make you believe in love, magic, and Neverland all over again.

"Any last words?"
"Go to hell, you freaking…filthy…godforsaken…"
Our noses almost touch as he dips his head and brushes a strand of my hair behind my ear. "Angel, the word you're looking for is pirate."

More books by Anna Katmore

ON THIN ICE
Counting Fireflies
Splintered North
*

Seventeen Butterflies

GROVER BEACH PLAYERS
Play With Me
Ryan Hunter
T Is For…
Dating Trouble
The Trouble with Dating Sue
The Impossible Bet
Taming Chloe Summers

CRUSHED HEARTS
Unfair Love
Broken Dawn
Awaking Trust

DREAMS OF NEVER EVER
Neverland
Pan's Revenge

WHISPERING PAGES
No Prince for Riding Hood
A Wolf in her Way

*

Eloyn
My Secret Vampire
You were my Fairy Tale

About the author

"I write stories because I can't breathe without."

Anna Katmore lives in an enchanting world of her own. It's a place where logic waits patiently at the gate and only dreamers are allowed to enter. Beware, though, once you step through, you may never wish to leave again.

Disney isn't just her passion; it's her attitude toward life. If she could, she'd wrap the world in a little stardust and save it from itself. Her patronus is a wolf. Her wand is a broken twig from an apple tree, 13¾ inches long, yet full of charm. And although there's always glitter on her shoes, she keeps a safe distance from Cinderella's glass slippers. Too risky, something might break.

For more magic, visit www.annakatmore.com